THE GRAMMARIANS

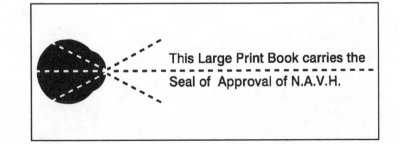

This Large Print Book carries the
Seal of Approval of N.A.V.H.

THE GRAMMARIANS

CATHLEEN SCHINE

THORNDIKE PRESS
A part of Gale, a Cengage Company

Farmington Hills, Mich • San Francisco • New York • Waterville, Maine
Meriden, Conn • Mason, Ohio • Chicago

Copyright © 2019 by Cathleen Schine.
Thorndike Press, a part of Gale, a Cengage Company.

ALL RIGHTS RESERVED
Thorndike Press® Large Print Basic.
The text of this Large Print edition is unabridged.
Other aspects of the book may vary from the original edition.
Set in 16 pt. Plantin.

**LIBRARY OF CONGRESS CIP DATA ON FILE.
CATALOGUING IN PUBLICATION FOR THIS BOOK
IS AVAILABLE FROM THE LIBRARY OF CONGRESS**

ISBN-13: 978-1-4328-7129-1 (hardcover alk. paper)

Published in 2019 by arrangement with Sarah Crichton Books, an
imprint of Farrar, Straus and Giroux

Printed in Mexico
1 2 3 4 5 6 7 23 22 21 20 19

To Janet

Twin, n. A couple; a pair; two
Twin, v.t. & i. To part, sever, sunder;
deprive (of)

*— Webster's New International Dictionary
of the English Language,* Second Edition

"That writer called," Michael said when she got home. "The young one."

"They're all young now, Michael. Be more specific."

"Why don't they call your assistant? I can't be expected to remember everything."

Her assistant? Daphne hadn't had an assistant since 2008. No one had assistants anymore. What was Michael thinking?

"She was rude," he was saying. "Peremptory."

"Ellen," Daphne said.

"Yeah, Ellen. She wants to talk to you about your sister."

Daphne went to the kitchen and filled a glass with ice and scotch. Her sister? Well.

"Ellen can go whistle Dixie," she said.

But Michael had gone back to his baseball game.

"The Yankees are a mean money team," she said.

"Honey, give it a rest."

Daphne sat and put her feet up on the ottoman. "What about my sister?"

"I don't know, Daphne. Something about an interview, a reunion, something. You told me to say no to everything about Laurel, so I said no. So I don't know." He put a finger to his lips. "I'm watching now."

"Yeah, yeah." She sipped the drink, stared at the TV without seeing it.

She had not heard from her sister, Laurel, in years. And now a flurry of calls.

"Flurry," she said softly. It was a word she and Laurel had both always liked.

CONVE´RSABLENESS. *n. s.* [from *convers-able*] The quality of being a pleasing companion; fluency of talk.
— *A Dictionary of the English Language*
by Samuel Johnson

They were late. It wasn't the first time, it wasn't even the first time that day, and she could sense time itself slipping. She wrapped her fingers around the bars. The bars were white and shiny. She could see them even in the dim light. With some effort she pulled herself up, then shook the bars until they rattled.

There was no response from the other side.

She shook the bars again. "Where are they? Where are they?"

Then the voice came. "They're late, as usual."

11

She shook the bars harder. She didn't like the dark, it kept what she loved away from her. It kept her alone.

"Although," the voice was saying, "if they're late 'as usual,' then that would be their usual time, and you can't really say they're late, can you?"

"You're a pedant," she said. "An insufferable pedant." But what she wanted to do was reach out and touch the voice, which belonged to her sister, to lie down beside her, feel the safety of her, warm and breathing. "Pedant," she said again, instead.

Her sister let out a long, shrill scream. "There. That ought to bring them running. Happy now?"

No, she was not happy now, she was bawling now. The screaming, though it blasted forth from her beloved sister, shocked her every time. She ought to have gotten used to it by now, but she had not.

"Oh, dry up," her sister said.

Which made her cry more. Her sister's scream did bring them running, as predicted, but somehow that made it worse, made her angry, and she banged her head against the bars in her rage.

By the time he lifted her, she was howling like a wolf. It wasn't until the bottle arrived that she was able to be calmed.

"You do get yourself worked up," he said. He kissed her, and she sucked on the bottle and let the milky sleep wash over her. His shirt smelled of laundry soap and there was the scent of wine on his lips. He walked to her sister's crib. "What if there were three of you?" he said gently as he picked her up, too, and held her in the crook of his other arm.

"See?" Her sister's voice was soft now. "It's okay now. Everything's okay."

And it was. Her sister was right. She was right so often.

She pushed the bottle to the side of her mouth and said thank you.

"More? Is that what you said, little Daphne?" He pushed the nipple back to the center of her mouth. "There we are."

Their mother came into the room with the other bottle of warm milk. She shook a few drops onto her wrist.

"Too hot," she said. "You'll have to wait just a minute, Laurel."

"No good deed goes unpunished," Laurel said, but the adults just smiled at her patience and good nature.

"Our feral little wolf twins," the father said.

"They do howl, it's true," their mother said. She took a baby, kissing its head.

13

"They want to make sure we hear them. They're very intelligent."

"One howls, then the second one howls even louder. It's as if one doesn't want to be left behind the other."

Their father bounced the baby he held almost frantically. He sang and paced, his arms aching with her small weight. "Are you Laurel or are you Daphne?"

"Oh, Arthur." But the next day their mother marked Laurel's toenail with a dab of scarlet nail polish.

It was difficult sometimes when both girls were red in the face and vibrating with infant rage.

"I wish I knew what they wanted," he said one night, holding the twins as his wife came in with the bottles, both properly warmed this time.

"Take a wild guess," the little girls cried out. "We want those bottles!"

"I think they're making themselves quite clear," their mother said, and she laughed. Though sometimes they unnerved Sally, too, chattering away in nonsense syllables as if it were a real language.

Their father exchanged a baby for a bottle, and the children were suddenly quiet, the only sounds their soft sucking and the creak of the upholstered rocking chair as their mother sank into it.

"Peace at last," she said, kissing the baby's head.

Their father continued to pace, back and forth across the small bedroom with its twin cribs, smiling down at the contented baby he held. I love you, he thought. Whichever the hell one you are.

Laurel was older by seventeen minutes. Daphne hated those seventeen minutes.

"I'll never catch up."

"It's not a race," their father said.

"Well, Laurel wins every race anyway."

"But you're smarter," Laurel said. She got tired of hearing about the seventeen minutes. Was it her fault she was older? And taller? And faster? That she came out first? The thought of "coming out" of their mother made her queasy. Why did everyone always bring it up, you came out first, you're the oldest because you came out first? "You're smarter, so shut up."

"You were alive for seventeen minutes without me. I was never alive without you."

"So?"

"So, I don't know. But you were."

Laurel did everything first. Everything good, everything bad. Laurel was first into the cold water at the beach, the first through

15

the door in nursery school and the first through the door of kindergarten. She would be first through the door of every classroom every year thereafter. She was the first into bed, the first one up in the morning.

"Laurel! Daphne! Go outside and play," their mother said. "It's nice out."

Laurel and Daphne. Two names for the same minor Greek goddess. But Uncle Don, who disliked them, sometimes called them Romulus and Remus Wolfe after the Roman twins suckled by a wolf, nicknames Sally hated. She did not like to think of herself as a hairy wolf. Sometimes Don just called them the Wolves.

"Yes, let them go howl in the woods," Uncle Don said.

"We revolt you," Laurel said, running past him.

"We are revolting," Daphne said. "Against you," she added.

They ran out the door, and the sun was sudden and white. They picked dandelions. The necklace Daphne made was too short and became a crown. A bee landed on it and she sat very still until it buzzed off. Laurel said, "Bee still," and they laughed and rolled down the hill until they felt sick.

"Let's go hear the Martinsons fighting,"

16

Laurel said. "I'll go first."

She wriggled into the crawl space under the neighbors' house. Daphne followed. It smelled sickly, of damp and dirt. Insects skittered away. A few footsteps creaked above them. A toilet flushed. Even the spiders' webs were dirty, powdered with fine silver dust and visible in the gloom. Mr. Martinson did not yell at Mrs. Martinson. Mrs. Martinson did not yell back. They could hear music from the television. *Million Dollar Movie.*

Daphne was the first to panic. She took a sudden shallow breath, her last, she thought, and she could not breathe in either direction, in or out. She clawed her way through the broken lattice and out of the crawl space, gasping. Behind her, she heard Laurel, her breath rasping, too. Laurel caught it, Daphne thought, like a cold or measles: she caught being afraid. She thought, At least I'm first in something, first at being scared. They lay on the grass, faces to the sun, light and air and warmth everywhere to rescue them. Their hearts beat more slowly. They were calm.

"Your two cowlicks were licked by the same cow," their father said. He smoked a cigarette on the porch and looked down at them fondly. They were hiding now. They often hid beside the front steps. They looked up at him. Laurel put a finger to her lips.

When their uncle came out he was already smoking his pipe. He was their father's brother. He was afraid of the twins. He said he was afraid for them, but they could tell they scared him. When they were in the same room he kept his eyes turned away. There's too much going on, their uncle said once, cocking his head in their direction.

Uncle Don believed that the twins should probably be raised apart so that each child could develop her own identity. He was the one who worried the most about their secret language. He said it was unnatural. He was a psychiatrist, so their mother and father had to pay attention to him.

That morning the girls had stood in front of him, side by side, while he read the Sunday paper, and stared.

"What is wrong with these two?" said Uncle Don, who never addressed them directly.

"Don, really," Sally said. "Is that how you talk to your patients?"

The girls began to sway together to the left, then the right, then again to the left.

"Jesus, what are they doing now?"

"Swaying," Laurel said.

"From side to side," Daphne added.

Their parents burst out laughing, but Uncle Don left the room.

"Paula!" he called to his wife. "We're leaving."

"I'm changing the baby," she yelled from the girls' bedroom. Brian, the baby, began to cry.

"Why are they in our room?" Laurel asked.

"Where would you like Aunt Paula to change the baby's diaper?" their mother said. "In the garage?"

"Uncle Don took the funnies with him," Daphne said.

Their father said they should not tease Uncle Don, and they would have to wait for the funnies.

Uncle Don didn't go home, he never did no matter how much they tormented him. Brian was taking a nap, he said, and could not be woken up, or Brian was awake and had to be rocked to sleep so he could take nap. Brian needed to be fed or Brian had just been fed and needed to be burped or had just burped and spit up and needed to be changed. Brian, as far as Laurel and Daphne could see, ran the show.

"He's so sticky," Laurel said to Aunt Paula, prodding Brian's cheek with a finger.

19

"Like an old lollipop," Aunt Paula said. She smiled at the girls. They once heard her tell their mother that they kept Uncle Don honest.

"What are your feral children doing now?" Don said as he stood on the porch with their father.

"We're hiding," Laurel said.

"Obviously," said Daphne.

"Kee-riste," said Uncle Don.

Daphne pulled a little notebook and pencil stub out of her pocket. She wrote "Kee-riste."

"They take notes?" Uncle Don said. "What are they, in the CIA?" He pointed the stem of the pipe at them, jabbing the air.

"I collect interesting words."

"I collect rocks," Laurel said, which was not true.

Their father put out his cigarette, and the two men went back inside.

"They're teasing you, Don," they heard their father say. "They're just children."

"Says you."

Because of Uncle Don, they had once been taken to a doctor who specialized in twins. The doctor disagreed with Uncle Don. He did not think twins should be raised apart.

20

He was tall and had cold, bony hands and white hair. The girls sat in small chairs at a small table with books and blocks to play with while their parents sat in two normal-sized chairs facing the doctor's desk. The windows were too high to look out of.

"De jers er dydnee," Daphne whispered.

"Jeedr ub. We won't be here long. Look, I drew a horse."

"The legs are kind of short."

"Drue, drue." And Laurel got a clean sheet to try again.

"When they were babies, Doctor, I honestly thought they were having conversations with each other," their mother said, "in their own language."

"Just baby talk," said their father.

The doctor said, "Many twins have a private language. It's natural, nothing to worry about. They outgrow it once they begin to speak properly."

"Oh, they do speak properly. Beautifully. They're five years old. They speak, they even read. They read the dictionary, Doctor. Then suddenly they'll be babbling in gibberish."

"It's nothing to worry about, Mrs. Wolfe," said the doctor. "They're lovely girls and they're developing beautifully. They'll outgrow the baby talk. You'll see."

"Deffjer," Laurel whispered to Daphne.
"Never," Daphne agreed.

SO´MEBODY. *n. s.* [*some* and *body.*] One; not nobody; a person indiscriminate and undetermined.
— *A Dictionary of the English Language*
by Samuel Johnson

Arthur Wolfe was not a big man. He was taller than his brother, Don, but that was like saying you were taller than Tom Thumb. Don was called Don Thumb throughout school. Maybe that was why Don was such a touchy son of a bitch. It was certainly the reason he became a psychiatrist — compensating. Just don't tell him that, Arthur thought. Dr. Wolfe, Dr. Don Thumb Wolfe, with his little beard that came to a little point. Arthur had never understood how someone so humorless could claim to uncover the secrets of another person's soul.

"What is a soul if not a repository of the absurd?" he asked Sally. "Expectations,

23

disappointments, grievances, good wishes."

"You should have been the doctor. You're the intellectual."

She meant it as a compliment, he knew that. It felt like a slap.

He was the intellectual. What good had that done him? For the intellectual of the family happened to be the older son, and the older son had been expected to take over the father's practice. Not as a doctor or a lawyer, that would not have been bad, but as an accountant. The work reminded him every day of his father, a man for whom money and its whereabouts, its taxation and exemption from taxation, was the alpha and the omega, the sun and the moon, the very stuff of life. Never had a man been so happy in his work. His father saw himself as a warrior in a constant battle against the IRS. Now he was old and could not even count his own pills.

"I do love a loophole," Arthur's father used to say, and Arthur, a small child, thought a loophole must be something delicious to eat, a special kind of candy.

He could not see the beauty of the puzzle as his father had. He had never been passionate about business or numbers. He had been forced to take accounting courses instead of poetry courses.

"Counting the coins of others," he said bitterly one night in April. "The filthy lucre of others. Piling it up, hiding it in safe, filthy little bundles. That's my profession."

"Filthy lucre." Sally smiled as she unbuttoned his wrinkled shirt and handed him his pajamas. He was worst in April, of course. Dark smudges beneath his eyes as if stained by piles of dirty gray cash, as if he'd been physically handling bills, counting them out with grubby hands and black fingernails. Sally said, "Don't be a snob about money, Arthur. Lawyers make money. Doctors make money."

"But they don't count money. Their days are not spent counting money."

"I wonder," she said, laughing.

He envied his brother's career as a psychiatrist. Reading myths all day? Listening to dreams? Pontificating about other people's sex fantasies? Don was like an oracle in a sulfurous cave. He, Arthur, was the dreamer of the family. He, Arthur, should be in the cave giving out prophesies. Not Don.

"We will have no numbers at the table," Arthur said when his wife or one of the twins brought up a subject that included money. The mention of a number of any kind was forbidden at dinner. Which only encouraged them.

"Would you like two potatoes or three, dear?" Sally would ask innocently. "You know, we had six inches of snow this month. But it was above thirty-two degrees, so it all melted."

When the girls wanted to annoy him they had only to chant, "There are two of us, two of us, two of us."

Two of them. He remembered bathing them when they were babies, so many pink arms and legs, so many chubby little hands splashing, two open little birds' mouths. He remembered leaning over the side of the tub, his shirtsleeves rolled up, his watch resting on the sink. He remembered dribbling water on their heads. And the crowns of their heads, the swirls of wet baby hair. He remembered the rush of tenderness so powerful he thought he might stop breathing.

When the girls first began to speak in their careful gibberish, Sally had worried.

"You just feel left out," he said.

She nodded. Yes, she did feel left out.

"Don't feel left out." He put his arms around her. "You're their mother."

"But they are . . ."

"What?"

"Each other."

He didn't like that, and he said so. They

were alike, two peas in a pod, but each pea had its own circumference. Daphne followed Laurel, a tiny acolyte. He wondered if Daphne would ever turn around and walk away. He wondered if Laurel would follow.

His brother had aggravated Sally's worry, getting her all worked up. But so what if they spoke in tongues? When he looked at his daughters, he found it difficult to see anything not lovely. He loved to watch them, to listen. Their voices were music, their little heads nodding at each other were dance.

"You should have been the shrink," his wife told him. "You have so much patience. When they talk to each other in gobbledegook, well, sometimes I feel like I'm going crazy."

Then, at last, they'd begun to speak English. Arthur had half expected their first words to be, like Macaulay's, "Madam, the agony is somewhat abated." In unison. But there was no dividing line, really, between their nonsense talk and their foray into English. Like foreigners living in Italy who quite unexpectedly realize one day that they can understand Italian, Arthur and Sally realized that they knew what their children were saying.

The prattle had become language, and

Sally no longer heard it as compelling background music. Every word was a word she could hear clearly and understand, a word that must be taken into account.

"Sometimes I feel like I'm going crazy!" she said. "They never stop talking!"

"Maybe," Arthur said, "you *are* going crazy. Maybe you just think they're speaking English. Maybe they're still speaking baby talk, and you are, too."

She laughed and sang, " 'Words, words, words! I'm so sick of words.' "

The twins were two little Professor Higginses. On rainy days, Sally listened to *My Fair Lady* over and over with them. They liked it better than any other record. "Why can't the English teach their children how to speak?" they sang. They jumped from the armchair to the couch, their arms spread, their bare feet flying. "Loverly!" they sang. "Ah-wooo-dent it be loverly." Tumbling over the back of the couch, running, leaping, flinging themselves into somersaults.

"Let a woman in your life and your serenity is through . . ."

Arms flailing, feet flying.

"When you yell you're going to drown . . ."

"I'll get dressed and go to town!"

Sally would sit in a chair in the corner, well out of their way, singing along.

28

"Somehow Keats will survive without you." What could they possibly make of that, the two little girls? They didn't know who Keats was. Or did they? Perhaps they had long ago memorized *Endymion* and recited it to each other at night, translated into their strange language.

"Do you know who Keats is?" she asked them one day.

"In the song?"

"Yes, in the song."

They both shrugged, and Laurel said, "He's in the song, Mommy."

"In the song," Daphne echoed.

"Silly," Sally heard Laurel say softly to her sister as they walked away.

"I know," Daphne whispered back. "Keats is in the song."

Sally put the record on for them then and relaxed into her chair in the corner. Her coffee was cold, of course. She was sure she had not had a hot cup of coffee since the girls had been born, but at least, she thought, sipping, tapping her foot to the music, her children did not know who Keats was.

Sally sometimes suggested other records. When the rain persisted and they couldn't go outside for several days in a row, they listened to *The King and I* or *Guys and Dolls*.

But *My Fair Lady* was the family background music.

Inevitably, somewhere around the time the rain began to fall in Spain, one of the girls would tire and trip, banging her head on the coffee table, and the crying would begin.

"Stop this fracas!" their mother would say in a voice of mock severity. They had only to hear the word "fracas" and they would cheer up and begin again.

BO´OKISH. *adj.* [from *book.*] Given to books; acquainted only with books. It is generally used contemptuously.
— *A Dictionary of the English Language*
by Samuel Johnson

In the evenings, the sisters waited for their father, kneeling on the couch, side by side, staring out the living room window.

"Maybe a wolf did suckle them when I wasn't looking," their mother said. "They have a canine sixth sense. They know when you're coming."

He suggested they bring him his slippers in their mouths, one slipper per.

"God, don't let them hear you. They'll really do it."

The night the dictionary arrived, they were there, on the couch, waiting. Their hands, like four paws, lined up along the back of the couch, their two chins resting on them. They were always mercifully silent at that time of day, Sally noticed, gazing into the dusk. Sniffing out their prey, she thought. She laughed, and they turned to look at her, two sweet and innocent faces. She leaned down, kissing one on the top of the head, then the other, in the blissful quiet that held them until Arthur came home.

The night the dictionary arrived, the girls heard the drawn-out crunching of gravel as they did every night, a favorite sound: the car in the driveway, their father. As adults, years and years later, they both particularly remembered that night. Happily watching their father step out of the car. The car door slamming shut. Another night. Daddy's home, Daddy's home. But then Daddy opened the trunk of the Buick and lifted out some sort of wooden stand. He lugged it into the house. No, no questions yet. Just wait and see. They stood on the front porch, then, cold bare feet, watching him lift an enormous book from the dark trunk of the car, like a doctor delivering a baby, they later said, the biggest book imaginable.

The stand was dragged into the new den. The biggest book imaginable was placed on top, open, each side swelling like a wave in the ocean.

Their mother said it looked like an altar.

"What's an altar?" Laurel said.

She didn't really care. And she knew what the word "altar" meant, somehow, without being told. But their father said, "Let's look it up."

He flipped through the biggest book imaginable, the dictionary, a book that contained and explained every word in the language, he said. The print was so small it looked like print for a mouse to read.

But the page that should have had the word "altar" was missing. Thousands of tissue-thin pages, and that one was lost, torn out, gone forever.

"Damn," he said.

Their mother laughed. "Look that up for the girls instead."

Daphne wanted him to close the big book. She wanted to run her hand along the cliff of compressed pages notched with steps the size of a fingertip, each one labeled with letters of the alphabet.

Other books were unloaded from the trunk of the car that night, but none of the other books had its own altar. A man who worked at their father's office had sold all the books to Arthur. The man's father had died, and the man had no use for his father's old books.

"You could say we've inherited them." Their father handled each one as if it were precious, breakable.

Laurel and Daphne watched their parents put the other books in the new, empty bookshelves. The den itself had just been constructed, converted from a small screened-in porch. Their parents admired how the new room looked. There were only thirty or so books, but they were impressive. Some were bound in leather.

It was an instant library. Like instant coffee or instant soup. That's what Uncle Don said. He said books were not meant for display, they were meant to be read.

Their father had been sitting comfortably in his new armchair in his new room, his legs stretched before him, pointing out the books to his brother. When Uncle Don said what he said, Arthur pulled his feet back. He no longer looked comfortable. One pant leg had risen up, and Laurel saw his skin, which looked uncomfortable, too, a strange colorless patch, vulnerable, almost frightened, like a squirrel waiting, frozen, on a branch until you passed by.

"Why not fill the shelves with your own books, books you'll really read?" Uncle Don said, as if answering their father, though their father had said nothing.

"We read them," Laurel said.

"Yes, well, they would, wouldn't they?" Uncle Don said. He pulled a volume from a shelf. "*The King's English*. Utterly appropriate for a five-year-old."

"Don't start up with them, Don," their father said, a little wearily.

"Yeah," Daphne said. "Don't start up with us."

She got a look from her father and said quickly, "Sorry, Uncle Don. Start up with us!"

That made their father laugh and Uncle Don look up at the ceiling and say, "God help us," which pleased Daphne. She looked at Laurel expecting a sly smile of approval. But Laurel was now sitting on the floor, her lips moving as she slowly read from *The King's English*.

" '. . . air of cheap or-na-ment . . .' "

They liked to pull the ottoman in front of the altar, climb up, and stand there, leafing through the dictionary. Sally sometimes encouraged them to watch television just to get them away from the dictionary. It couldn't be healthy, two little faces pecking at the musty pages of a dead man's discarded book. Of course, it was educational, she told herself that. But what sort of an education? Bits and scraps, words as unconnected to one another as candy wrappers dropped on the street. She smiled at that thought. A lot of candy wrappers that would be, thousands. Where had the thousands of pieces of candy gone? Sally went to the dresser in the front hall and opened a drawer. She always kept a box of chocolates there in case someone stopped in for coffee. If the children wanted to read about words, why shouldn't they? She went into the kitchen, made a cup of coffee, and opened the box. She extracted two pieces heavy with caramel and nuts. But just two. They were quite rich.

Collie, colie, coaly, coal-black. See COAL. 1. A large dog of a breed originating in Scotland, where it has been used for generations in herding sheep. The breed is large, standing 20 to 24 inches at the shoulder and weighing 50 to 60 lbs. The variety with a rough and profuse coat is more common and decidedly more commanding than the smooth-haired variety.

In the frail, almost transparent pages, the collie looked like Lassie and was indeed commanding. On other pages there were other dogs drawn in fine-lined profiles. There was a long, low dachshund, decidedly less commanding than even the smooth-haired collie, and a seriously uncommanding dog with a fanciful name, the Dandie Dinmont terrier.

"And spaniels, spaniels, spaniels," Laurel said. "Every spaniel has its own drawing."

She brought this up with her father one night after dinner.

"Why isn't the dictionary nice to cairn terriers? It gives them no picture. And look what it says about them: *employed chiefly to enter rock piles and dislodge vermin.*"

"Vermin." Not a nice word. And while other dogs were described as "noble" and "loyal," cairns were "employed."

"The dictionary is not fair."

"I don't think it's supposed to be fair, exactly," their father said.

"It's not supposed to be mean, is it?"

"Well, it has mean words in it, so we can understand them and know what they mean, but . . ."

"How can 'mean' mean *mean* and also mean *mean*?" Laurel said.

"Perhaps we should get the girls a real dog," Sally said that night when she got into bed. "They spend so much time looking up

37

breeds in the dictionary, maybe a flesh-and-blood dog would do them good."

"It's you who wants a dog," Arthur said. "Isn't it? Two wolf pups not enough?"

How did he know? Could he tell she was lonely?

Sally Wolfe loved her daughters as much as her husband did, but she was less comfortable with them. She loved them the way you love the birds in the trees, that was the sensation: the birds sing, they flutter, their colors flash by; but you cannot touch them because you cannot catch them. She admired her children from a baffled distance, pretty little girls, as busy as birds, as alien. She worried about Daphne and Laurel, too, worried about how they would fit in, because they seemed to fit nowhere but with each other.

Sally was a dominating mother, when she could be, but it was all in self-defense, which was something the twins clearly understood.

When she told them bedtime stories, they listened intently, then commented, like adults exiting a play.

"That was not a good ending," Laurel said.

"It doesn't make sense, Mommy, and it's a little boring because the bear never finds the honey anyway. And what bear would be friends with a spider? Spiders don't have friends."

"It's a story, girls. In stories anyone can be friends with anyone else. And how do you know spiders don't have friends?"

They thought about that for a while, until Laurel said, "No." She shook her head back and forth on the pillow. "Uh-uh."

There was such finality. Sally didn't know whether to laugh or beg forgiveness. That was often how she felt with the girls.

"Tell us another." Daphne was sitting up now.

"If my stories are so bad, why do want another?" Sally asked. "That's silly, you sleepy girls."

"We're silly," said Daphne.

Sally gave a sigh. They liked to make her words circle back on her.

"You can do it, Mommy," Laurel said. "I know you can." She gave her an encouraging nod.

Sally waited, counted to two, and there it was: "*We* know you can," Daphne added, just as Sally had expected. She smiled at the two serious faces. Not only would she tell another story, she knew, but she would try harder.

"Good one," Daphne whispered at the

end. She was almost fully asleep.

"Thank you, Mommy," Laurel said.

Sally left them, elated with her success.

Arthur came home with a puppy a week later, an Irish setter mix the color of the girls' hair, a bumptious, friendly creature who settled on Sally as his mistress the moment he galloped through the kitchen door. He slept on the rug on Sally's side of the bed. He followed her, dogged her, as she liked to say, from room to room, his scarlet ears flopping, his nose reaching up reverently to graze her hand. If the dog was by a closed door, it meant that Sally was somewhere on the other side of that door. He listened when she told the twins stories, without comment or criticism of her narrative skills. The girls — inevitably, Sally thought — named the puppy Webster.

HARMONICK. *adj.* [. . . *harmonique,* French.] Portioned to each other; adapted to each other; concordant; musical.

— *A Dictionary of the English Language*
by Samuel Johnson

If you can fold something, and both sides match up, that thing has symmetry. Twins are symmetrical. Beauty of form arising from balanced proportions — far preferable to one dictionary's definition of "twins" that they'd seen: *One of two children or animals born at the same time.* It was practically agricultural. The example of a sentence using "twins" was worse: *Experiments were carried out using sets of identical twins.*

Were Laurel and Daphne experiments? Farm experiments gone wrong?

When the dog was with them, a real

animal, his tail swinging gaily in the sun, his ears rising and falling with his gentle trot, the girls did not feel like an experiment; they felt like a parade. People smiled and greeted them and made much of the three redheads in an open, good-natured way. The red-haired dog, because he was a dog, made the redheaded twins less identical, less strange. When it was just the two of them, each face a mirror of the other, their clothes carefully chosen to match, their long, dark red hair flaming behind them, they became, again, oddities.

People often stared at them. To be the object of that fleeting stare, a series of those stares as you walk down the street, makes you wonder what is wrong. You hold your sister's hand and the heads turn, eyes following you, one after another, a row of faces flipping as you pass, like pages in a book. What do they see? You look out from your eyes, you burn with shame, but you don't know what you're ashamed of because you can't see what they see. Then you turn and see your sister. She, also a mortified pink, has turned to you. And you know then that what they see is identical to the person you see, the person you love the best. And then you change the way you walk. You swagger. And then you are beautiful and symmetrical, two lovely girls walking hand in hand, two sides of the folded paper, shapely as origami, mysterious, confident, radiant. You are not an animal or an experiment. You are math. You are perfection.

Then your sister turns a new, funny shade of pink that is really a shade of green. She says she isn't feeling well. She says she must have eaten too much candy at the movies. Your mother says, I told you so. Your sister's hand is clammy and your sister is green. She is bent over the curb throwing up.

You stand away from her, and she alone absorbs all the stares now. The piece of origami paper has unfolded, is flat, torn. One half of the sheet of paper vomits in the gutter. The other half wants to disappear but also thinks, At least my shoes don't have throw-up on them.

When you get home, you both have fevers. Soon you are told you both have measles. You lie in your twin beds with the curtains drawn. Even in the dim light, you can see that the red spots do not occur on the same places on your otherwise identical bodies and faces. You conclude, with the sharp intelligence of a child, that you are not symmetrical in sickness. It seems profound. And sad. And it is a lesson you will not forget.

In the darkened room, you tell each other

stories. Your parents have read *Twelfth Night* to you because it is cultural and educational and has twins in it. You argue about which of you would be which, both of you wanting to be Viola, neither wanting to be a boy dressed as a girl. Neither of you wanting to be named Sebastian. You work out an agreement, a plot change that requires even more disguises and changes of identities than the play, but you both become testy and exhausted and feverish and cannot follow your own script and argue again until you fall into a disturbed, overheated sleep, your hand stretched across the narrow divide between your beds holding fast to your sister's hand.

"What if the blue I see is different than the blue you see?" one of you says in the morning.

"The blue is the same, and our eyes are the same. So no way," says the other of you.

Twins in literature are always disguised as each other, or they are sleeping with each other. The banality of "twin sweater sets" cannot make up for Siegmund and Sieglinde. You think that later, of course, much later, when no one wears sweater sets anymore and you have just read a disturbing story by Thomas Mann.

"But what if we both call it blue and it's

44

really a different color but we both have always called it blue so we think we're seeing the same color but we're not?" says one of you.

"Blue is blue," the other of you says.

"What I see as blue might be what you see as green. We don't know. You're not in my eyes. I'm not in your eyes."

"The sky is the same color whatever you say."

"Well, that's true. But I might say it's green."

"Do you?"

"Of course not. It's blue."

On and on the arguments go.

Identical twins, dressed in identical outfits — are they half or double? It's pleasant to make people uncomfortable sometimes, people like your uncle. Making other people uncomfortable allows you to shake off your own discomfort. When people stare at you, you stare back, four matching eyes.

You have dark red wavy hair and round, childlike faces. Even as children, your faces are not so much children's faces as childlike faces, an approximation, a description, a suggestion rather than a definition. It is difficult to notice your faces beyond that, partly because of the dazzling red hair but mostly because there are two of you. You understand this when you are older, when someone brings too many gifts to a birthday party or too many bottles of good wine to a dinner party, and the presents and the wine are undervalued in their own abundance. You are indistinct, undervalued in your own abundance.

Sometimes you wish you knew other twins or had siblings who were twins, like the Bobbsey Twins.

There was one time when Laurel cut her own hair in an attempt to look different from Daphne. Your mother was furious and took you both to the beauty parlor to get identical pixie haircuts. Daphne cried herself to sleep that night, her back turned to her sister.

"I'm sorry," Laurel said, poking her. "I'm sorry you had to get an ugly haircut because of me."

Daphne did not answer. She secretly liked the pixie cut.

"It will grow back," Laurel said.

"Shut up."

"I'm sorry, Daphne. I said I was sorry." She yelled into Daphne's ear: "I'm SORRY!"

"Shut up. I don't care what you do. So shut up." But then she thought, You think the haircut's ugly and you're stuck with it, which made her feel better. And you still look just like me, which made her feel better still.

In school, both Laurel and Daphne often had to clarify that they were themselves and not their sister. "No," they would say. "I'm the other one."

"I'm the other one," Daphne said in third grade when a little boy who had a crush on Laurel stuck paste in her hair. "I'm the other one."

"I don't care," the boy said, but he ran away to the far end of the playground.

"I'm the other one," Laurel said to the cafeteria lady who knew Daphne's love of Sloppy Joes and was ladling an extra gelatinous spoonful onto her hamburger bun.

The cafeteria lady said, "Oh! Well, you enjoy your meal, too, dear."

"How can we both be the other one?" Daphne asked Laurel.

They looked up "other" in the dictionary. The entry was surprisingly long. "Other" was an adjective that meant *one of two.* It was usually preceded by a demonstrative or possessive word. Daphne liked the idea of a demonstrative word, imagining the word hugging and kissing "other," generally making a spectacle of itself, until their father explained that a demonstrative word meant, simply, a word like "this" or "that."

"Other" also meant *additional.*

" 'Additional' — that means *not the main one, not the important one,*" Daphne said.

"Yes, but they mean it as *different.* See? It says *different.* And *not the same.*"

"Not the same is the same as *different."*

Laurel squinted at more of the tiny print. "Two obsolete meanings!" she said. Obsolete meanings were a find — like the time they discovered a chamber pot in their grandparents' attic. Obsolete meanings were treasures of infinite value and no use.

Daphne got out her notebook and pencil.

"One of the obsolete meanings is *left,*" Laurel said, her face close to the page, her nose touching it.

"Left like your left hand? Or left like left behind, left over?"

"Hand."

What a wonderful, mysterious word. "Other." It not only took a pronoun, it *was* a pronoun. It was also an adverb. And a conjunction!

"It's even a noun," Laurel said. She read:

" 'Other, n. Philos. That which exists as an opposite of, or as excluded by, something else; as, the nonego is the other of the ego, nonbeing the other of being, the objective world is the other of self-consciousness.' "

"I'll be the ego," Daphne said.
"I'll be the objective world."
And they ran off to play.

It would be difficult to fault Sally for an occasional feeling of inferiority when she contemplated her children. There they stood, when they stood still, vibrant and loquacious and cocksure. Their red hair marked them as different and as the same, as other. Their flaming bright heads stood out in any group of children, so unlike the girls and boys with blond, brown, black hair; the two of them identical in their contrast. They seemed to their mother, sometimes, to be mythical creatures, beyond the reality of skinned knees and squabbles, dirt-smeared tears, or even laughter. But then one of them would skin her knee and the dirt and tears and need were as real as anybody else's, and Sally would almost welcome the unhappy moment, which was a moment she could share with one injured daughter, unencumbered by the other. She asked Arthur's brother, Don, if that was selfish of her. He was a pompous ass, as Arthur often pointed out, but so were the children, as she often tried to explain to Arthur. And Don was a psychiatrist. That had to count for something. Or did it? He sat her down at the kitchen table as if the kitchen were his office and spoke soberly about archetypes.

"Romulus and Remus Wolfe," he began. He chuckled. "Sorry about the pun."

He clamped his pipe between his teeth and puffed in what Sally considered a derisive manner, his chin tilted up, his eyes looking down at her. "Romulus and Remus Wolfe," he said again. As always, she thought not of two boys nursing from a she-wolf but of two wolf cubs nursing from her. Still, there was nothing wrong with a pun. Don was a snob. So was Arthur, of course. But only about filthy lucre.

Don was now telling her about Jacob and Esau. But they weren't twins, were they? One was hairy and one was smooth. That was all she could remember. Now Don was talking about the sun and the moon. Twins were antagonistic, he said. They were mystical and primary and opposite and one.

Sally poured him a glass of iced tea as he spoke. She thought of Thompson and Thomson, the detective twins in the *Tintin* comics, and she wanted to laugh. Instead, she silently passed Don a plate of cookies. She was sorry she had asked him about the girls. She felt foolish now. Jung was all right, but she had two little girls, she was not a wolf, she was not the sun or the moon or Leda or the swan. She was not biblical. She was tired. She was outgunned. She said, "I know you're right, Don. But what's all that got to do with me? How do you raise archetypes?"

Don laughed, not his normal sarcastic, superior laugh that soured the air around him. He gave a full, open laugh, and for a moment he reminded Sally of Arthur. "The same way you raise every other kid," he said. "By the seat of your goddamn pants."

Years later, when the girls were grown, Sally had occasion to remember Don's words. She was sitting on the couch with Daphne, holding Daphne's newborn baby, Prudence. Sally began to sing to the baby:

Tweedle, tweedle, tweedle dee.

She had sung that song to Laurel and Daphne every night.

I'm as happy as can be.
Jimminy Cricket, Jimminy Jack,
You make my heart go clickety-clack.

"I used to think that Laurel was Tweedledee," Daphne said. "I couldn't wait for the last lines when you'd finally sing Tweedledum. That was me. Tweedledum."

51

She moved closer to her mother and her daughter.

" 'Look at that sugar plum,' " Daphne sang.

Sally thought, I did something right. She took her daughter's hand and held it, hard.

BA'BERY. *n.s.* [from *babe.*] Finery to please a babe or child.

      — *A Dictionary of the English Language*
                    by Samuel Johnson

Uncle Don and Aunt Paula and their little boy, Brian, came for dinner every other Sunday; and every other Sunday, Laurel and Daphne and their parents went to Uncle Don and Aunt Paula and Brian's house for dinner. This Sunday was a home gathering for Laurel and Daphne, which they much preferred. Because Brian was afraid of the dog, they spent a large part of the visit brushing Webster as a way to keep their distance from their younger cousin. He was little and petulant and too easy to tease.

At the dinner table, Uncle Don told their father to tell them to stop babbling, which made them talk faster and interrupt each other more.

"Babbling!" cried Daphne. "That's ono-matopoeia!"

"Spell 'onomatopoeia'!"

Brian stuck out his lower lip ominously and muttered, "Dumb."

"Foolish!" Laurel called out.

"Speechless!" yelled Daphne.

"God, yes, speechless," Uncle Don said.

"Thunderstruck!" Laurel and Daphne said at the same time.

Aunt Paula gave a small laugh. "You girls."

Brian said, "Girls are dumb. Girls have chinas."

"Hush," said Aunt Paula, still smiling a little.

"Brian!" Uncle Don said. "No china talk at the table."

"They do have chinas," said Brian. "They do."

He looked accusingly at the twins.

Uncle Don looked accusingly at Aunt Paula.

"Nolo contendere," said Aunt Paula, who was a lawyer.

"China, china, china," Brian chanted.

"We've been talking about possibly having another baby, explaining things, in case we ever do," Uncle Don shouted over the din. "Jealousy. Perfectly natural," he added.

"Why bring it up unless it's happening?"

Arthur asked.

"That's what I said," Paula said.

"Precautionary."

"In case you forget precautions," said Sally.

They all laughed, except Don, his yowling son, and the baffled twins.

"CHINA . . ."

Brian was eight years younger than the girls. He had been a pleasing baby, looking slowly around him, his mouth open. But as a four-year-old, he left something to be desired. He still looked slowly around him, his mouth was still open, but the behavior and the aspect of a gentle baby were no longer becoming in a little boy. And since the age of two he had thrown tantrums, which disrupted most dinners and outings the two families shared. He screamed when he saw Webster, he pulled the twins' hair, and they were, being older, forbidden to retaliate.

"His early interest in bodily functions has clearly advanced to an interest in body parts," Arthur said.

"Take your cousin out to play," their mother said. "Distract the child."

"I'm a child, too," Laurel said. "And I'm not done eating."

"Me, too," said Daphne. "Me, either."

"I don't want to go outside with them!" Brian screamed. "They have chinas."

"I told you not to use euphemisms," Uncle Don said to his wife.

"That hardly seems to be the issue," she said. "And it's not a euphemism. It's baby talk."

"I'm not a baby!" Brian screamed. "I'm not a baby!"

Daphne and Laurel caught a beseeching look from their mother and lured their cousin outside with the promise of squashing ants. There were no anthills available, so they sat in the driveway and threw pebbles. He seemed to like that.

"You're freaks," he said. "Freaks of nature. Daddy said."

"*She* is," Laurel said, pointing at Daphne. "But I'm not."

"Nope. *She* is the freak of nature," Daphne said, pointing at Laurel.

"Do you know what a freak is, Brian?"

Brian shook his head. "No."

"It means princess," Daphne said.

"A princess who can fly."

"Fly where?" Brian asked.

"To China."

Brian smirked. "You said a bad word. I'm telling Daddy."

"Don't be a tattletale, Brian."

"I'm telling Daddy you called me a tattle-tale."

"Do you know what 'tattletale' means, Brian?"

"Yes."

"Do you know what 'tattle' is?"

"No."

"Then how can you know what 'tattletale' means?"

Brian put a pebble in his mouth and pondered this.

"A bad word?" he said at last.

Laurel and Daphne congratulated him with such warmth and sincerity that he decided not to tell his father anything. There was hope for him, they told Brian.

"There's hope for me," he told his parents when they went back inside. "Because 'tattle' is a bad word." He began chanting, "Tattle, tattle, tattle!"

Aunt Paula said, "Maybe one child is enough."

"The next one might be easier," Sally said.

"You never know," Arthur said.

They all looked at Brian, standing on a chair chanting, "Tattle, tattle, tattle!"

"Sweet Jumping Jesus," said Uncle Don. He shook his head in a kind of awe.

SCRINE. *n.s.* [*scrinium,* Latin.] A place in which writings or curiosities are reposited.
— *A Dictionary of the English Language*
by Samuel Johnson

These are some of the words Daphne collected in her notebook:

fugacious
rebarbative
oxters
divagations
promptuary
whilom
irenicon
hendiadys
aposiopesis
gloze
turgid
conurbation

She read through books understanding practically nothing of the content, on the lookout only for words she fancied.

"But the words don't have to be fancy," she explained to her mother. "I have to fancy them. That means I have to like them."

"But how do you know you like them if you don't know what they mean?"

Daphne could not explain something so basic, so primal. How do you know a flower is pretty? How do you know a cat's fur is soft?

Laurel was the one who looked the words up. How could Daphne stand it, not knowing the meaning, just guessing from the context of sentences she didn't really understand? It was ridiculous when there was always a simple answer. That was her job, to look up the word in the tissue-paper pages of the dictionary and record the meanings in the notebook.

Each word, once it landed in the notebook and was defined with its dictionary definition and spoken out loud by the sisters, seemed to develop its own special personality. "Whilom" and "oxters" were such different characters, their temperaments arising from their looks, their sound, and to a lesser extent their meaning. "Whilom": *former.* "Oxters": *armpits.* "Whilom" was light and airy and lost, like a lady in a white nightgown wandering through a field of flowers filmed over with dewdrops; "oxters," drudging and heavy and tired, muscled and damp with sweat. Sometimes Whilom and Oxters met in the flowery field. Irenicon might appear between them then, an offering of peace as cool and placid as a river, Whilom dipping a bare foot into the calm water, Oxters immersing its entire self with a groan of relief. Laurel and Daphne loved their collection. They played with the words as if they were toys, mental toys, lining them up, changing their order, and involving them in intrigues of love and friendship and bitter enmity.

They tried to include their younger cousin Brian in their game, but his participation was fugacious.

"It is not," he said when they told him this, and ran, as usual, to tell his parents that the twins had called him a bad name.

"It means *fleeting,*" Laurel said when Uncle Don complained in turn to their parents and their father confronted them.

"You made him cry. He's just a little boy. He doesn't understand."

They were forced to apologize to Brian

and play Go Fish with him. They let him win.

"We're sorry we were mean. We didn't mean to be."

"Don't start," their father said. "Don't start that with him."

The adults were drinking cocktails, and the children sat around the coffee table with their cards.

Uncle Don said, "Their regret was pretty damn fugacious, too, wasn't it?"

Brian began to cry again.

"Don't cry, Brian. It's just a word," Daphne said. "It means *it's gone away.* Like, if you stop crying, you can say your crying was fugacious. And if you say the word three times, it's yours, right, Daddy?"

"All yours."

But Brian sniffled and said he didn't want any stupid words, he would prefer to play Go Fish again.

"More words for us," Daphne whispered to Laurel, but both girls were disappointed. They wanted to like their cousin Brian, but what would become of someone who understood so little of what mattered in the world?

The twins argued not just with Brian or Uncle Don. They argued with each other every day. And slept in the same bed every night. Their parents had gotten two twin beds, but every morning they found the girls in the same bed, arms around each other.

"They're called twin beds, girls," their mother said. "Two beds for two twins."

But, until junior high school, they insisted on sleeping together. Then one night Laurel said, "Well, I think I'll just sleep in my own bed tonight."

Daphne looked at her sister. "Need a little privacy?"

Laurel actually blushed. "I didn't say that."

Daphne shrugged. "Dar vudge obe dzegs, deedr." *The force of sex, dear.*

"I didn't say anything about sex!"

"You don't have to. Privity speaks louder than words." It was one of their favorite words. Laurel found it in Dr. Johnson's dictionary. Its meaning was: *private communication, joint knowledge.* But in the plural it meant *private parts.* " 'Privity' and 'privities,' " Daphne said.

"I never said 'privities.' "

"Shared DNA, Laurel. It speaks volumes. I know all your secrets."

Laurel began to laugh. "DNA has a big mouth. And a big nose!" She tapped her nose, which she complained about constantly.

"I like our nose," Daphne said.

"Be my guest," said Laurel.

"But that means you think I'm ugly."

Laurel said, "I get to have an opinion about my own nose."

They squabbled a bit more, then turned out their lights.

"Peace, love, and DNA," Laurel whispered.

They both had simultaneously, that minute, added "DNA" to their shared vocabulary without having to consult each other. "Masturbation" was not a word they would ever have used, even with each other.

For their thirteenth birthday, Laurel and Daphne received a portable record player and a copy of *Revolver* to play on it. Their father also gave them a book entitled *The New Guide of the Conversation in Portuguese and English.*

"It will make you laugh," he said when they unwrapped it.

They looked uncertainly at the little paperback.

"It's a phrase book," he said. "From the nineteenth century."

"But we don't really want to learn Portuguese, do we, Daphne?"

Daphne shook her head.

"Don't worry," Arthur said. "You won't!"

They opened the book.

" 'Proverbs,' " Laurel read.

Daphne read: " 'The stone as roll not heap up not foam.' "

" 'To make at a stone two blows'!" Laurel read.

" 'It before that you marry look twice'!"

" 'The mountain at work put out a mouse'!"

The girls were in full cry. Arthur watched them and thought, God, I love them.

He said, "It was all the rage in Victorian England. Mark Twain was a fan, too. The translations are so preposterous, it became a comic sensation. It was known as *English as She Is Spoke.*"

" 'That which feels one's snotly blow one's nose.' "

"This is a new edition," Arthur said. "Brendan Gill wrote the introduction." Arthur worshipped the *New Yorker* critic. He worshipped *The New Yorker* generally. He kept all the back issues stacked neatly in the den.

"You know you'll never read all these," his brother, Don, said now at the mention of Brendan Gill. He gestured toward the piles of magazines. "They're just gathering dust."

"I might go back to an article. You never know."

Don made a dismissive sound.

"Uncle Don said 'Puh,' " Laurel said loudly to Daphne.

"Puh," Daphne said with great emphasis on the *p:* "Puh."

"They have never liked me," Uncle Don said to their father.

"No one likes you, Don," Arthur replied. "You're unlikable. You know that."

"Puh," said Don.

The twins retreated happily to their room to listen to *Revolver* and read aloud to each other from the little phrase book:

" 'Here is a horse who have a bad looks'!"

" 'He not sail know to march, he is pursy, he is foundered'!"

" 'Take care that he not give you a foot's kick'!"

"But do you ever worry that they don't have that many friends?" Arthur said to his wife one night.

Sally smiled at the "but." Nothing, no conversation or observation, had preceded Arthur's question. He must have been turning it over in his mind.

"They have friends," she answered. "Of course they do."

"Not that many."

"How many friends do they need? They have each other."

Laurel did eventually have a best friend, a slender, dreamy girl named Linda with long black hair and enormous blue eyes. Linda was a liability in some ways, so beautiful and otherworldly that any boy Laurel had her eye on had eyes only for Linda. One summer, she and Laurel were counselors at a day camp the town started for disadvantaged children. By disadvantaged they meant black. Linda played the guitar and sang folk songs. Laurel watched the children yawn and fidget while Linda crooned. The songs were beautiful. Linda had written them herself. They were about justice and rivers and death.

"And she looks just like Joan Baez or Buffy Sainte-Marie when she sings," Laurel told Daphne. "But the children act like they're in school with a horrible, boring teacher."

It was only then that Daphne realized how jealous she was of Linda and that she knew she didn't have to be jealous at all. She could already hear the Linda fatigue in Laurel's voice. Linda was mentioned less and less at the dinner table. When she was, it was no longer because Linda was reading a book by Alan Watts or was boycotting wine because it was made with grapes. It was because Linda didn't notice when one of the children wandered away from the playground.

"And you know," Laurel added, to her sister's satisfaction, "it's not as if she even drinks wine, she's not eighteen, not that that stops anyone, but she doesn't drink, so that was not much of a sacrifice, when you think about it."

"It won't help Cesar Chavez, anyway," Sally said. "Wrong grapes."

"Thank god," Arthur said. He had given up table grapes without much resistance when the girls demanded their parents join the boycott. But wine was another matter. "And what do you mean, being underage doesn't stop anyone? It stops you, I hope."

Both girls rolled their eyes and made their awful *tsk* sound.

"You're such a hypocrite," Laurel said.

"That is my right as an adult."

"It's Linda who's the real hypocrite," Daphne said.

"What happened to the lost camper?" Sally asked. "That's the real point."

"She's not a hypocrite. She's very dedicated."

Daphne realized she had made a strategic

mistake, but she could not stop. "She's so dedicated she lost a kid."

"She didn't lose him. He was in the boys' room. Why are you all ganging up on Linda?"

If it had been Daphne, she would have stormed away from the table, but her sister didn't storm. Which enraged Daphne. "Well, if you care about her so much —"

"Okay, girls, that will do," Sally said. "The little boy was found, no one eats grapes, your father and I can drink our wine with a clear conscience, and no one is perfect."

Daphne stormed away from the table.

In five minutes, she returned. "I'm still hungry."

Laurel gave her the as-yet-ungnawed bone from her lamb chop. A peace offering of blackened fat. Scraping the fat from the bone with her teeth, Daphne smiled a greasy smile of thanks.

COLLECTI′TIOUS. *adj.* [*collectitius*, Lat.]
Gathered up.
— *A Dictionary of the English Language*
by Samuel Johnson

Every other Sunday, the twins were on their front lawn waiting when Brian and his mother and father roared up in their old Citroën, a car that was, to Brian's mind, as affected as his father's pipe and goatee. Laurel and Daphne called the car the See-tro-eh. "See-tro-eh," they would chant, cartoon French accents, kissing their fingers like a cartoon chef. Don would curse softly and bring the car to a stop with a jolt. Brian was embarrassed by the Citroën, by the twins' reaction to it, but he secretly loved it, its odd shape and the way it sighed back down on its wheels when the motor stopped. The twins could See-tro-eh the car all they wanted, but they always asked him how it felt when the car rose on its haunches or fell back to earth. They always begged their uncle for a ride.

"Children who are not mature enough to appreciate a vintage Citroën do not ride in a vintage Citroën," Don would say, not to the girls, but to Brian's mother.

Brian would have liked to lord this refusal over his cousins, but there was no spirit of superiority for him in his father's snub. Brian was too intimate with weakness not to recognize it in someone else, and he knew fear when he saw it. His father was afraid of the two little girls. So was Brian.

He was ignored by his cousins, mostly. When they came to his house with their parents on alternate Sundays, Brian always asked them to play in the woods with him. He loved the woods surrounding his house and spent most of his free time there.

"There are bears in the woods," Daphne said. "Let's play Scrabble."

"There haven't been bears here since 1776," he said. He had no idea when the last bear had been seen in Larchmont, or if there ever had been bears.

For a moment, he thought he had impressed them. But they both shrugged and Laurel said, "How do you know?"

"Look it up," he said, which was enough

70

to get them to follow him along a swampy trail that led to the beach, where they saw a deer swimming along the shore.

Paula thought: The two parts of the Wolfe family are small and inverted, if that was the right word — the opposite of extended. And oppressively close. She wondered why Don, who saw dysfunction everywhere, did not see that. Don and Arthur were like trees that had been planted too near each other, their crowded roots popping up from the soil naked and exposed. They were worst, the most gnarled and raw, when they were together. Don was to blame, she thought. He was cruel to his brother. Even the dog noticed, sidling protectively up to Arthur the minute Don entered the same room.

"Why do you insist on seeing them every weekend if they bother you so much?" Paula asked Don. That was many years ago, when the twins were little and babbling their strange language at each other. "Why does he want you to come? You're cruel to him. And you're not a cruel man."

Don had scowled and said, "Thanks for the vote of confidence."

She never could figure the two brothers out, but she hadn't minded the visits. The predictability, the rhythm; every weekend, a

71

visit by one family to the other family. As time went on, Paula came to consider Sally her best friend, which made it easier, almost amusing, when the brothers would squabble. The two women would share a glance, a suppressed smile.

Brian's father often said that Arthur was too dull for someone of Sally's nervous imagination. But as Brian got a little older he realized that Arthur was too peculiar to be dull. No numbers at the dinner table! he would shout. The girls would stand on their chairs and chant numbers until Arthur pushed his chair back with a crash and chased them from the room, their shrieks of laughter trailing like colorful scarves. Don said his brother was neurotic, thwarted, and therefore explosive. Don had a diagnosis for everyone. Brian's mother called him Diagnosis Don, which made him almost as angry as Uncle Arthur pretended to be.

Brian had once tried, at the dinner table, to express his own love of numbers to Uncle Arthur. Admittedly, he was showing off for his cousins, home from college, superior beings more superior than ever.

"You're young," Arthur had said.

Brian, disappointed he had not gotten a rise out of his uncle, tried again. "There are patterns," he said. "Beautiful patterns. The patterns of nature, of the universe —"

"Shut up, darling," Brian's mother said in her smiling, gentlest voice. She often told Brian to shut up in that voice. It was one of the intimacies between them that Brian's father disliked.

"Don't say 'shut up' to the boy," Don said.

"Yes, it will stunt my growth, Mother."

"I just want some peace," Uncle Arthur said. He put his hand out, still holding a large ear of corn, and patted Brian's hand with his wrist, the corncob waving above like a sword. "Peace."

"Numbers," Don said, "are cold but necessary."

Did he expect his wife to say, "Shut up, darling," in her special Shut-up-darling voice?

"Like men," she said instead.

"Cold but necessary," Daphne chimed in. "Like ice cream."

"Or shrimp cocktail," said Laurel.

"Or beer," said Arthur.

Don said, "Damn it." He pushed his plate away.

"Well, one cold thing I detest is coffee," Sally said. "And cold coffee is not at all necessary." She and Paula took the plates off the table and retreated into the kitchen to get the coffee and dessert. Brian heard cups rattling and quiet laughter. He wanted to join them, to also escape the two pontificating men and the merciless twins. But he sat, paralyzed as he so often was by his father's displeasure.

"The ocean," he said after a while.

They all looked at him.

"Cold," he said. "But necessary."

FLAGRA′TION. *n.s.* [*flagro,* Latin.] Burning.
— *A Dictionary of the English Language*
by Samuel Johnson

Laurel and Daphne had always argued about something. They argued out of habit — bored, lackadaisical arguments that had the slow, fated rhythm of playing Solitaire. Until Daphne retreated in a huff.

"If you do it bit by bit, you tan instead of burning," Laurel said. It was a hot day at the end of June and they had just finished their junior year of high school. Laurel was lying on her stomach on a beach towel in the backyard. The sun beat down on her, on her legs, on her head. She was wearing a bikini, but she had undone the strap of the top so there would be no tan line. Daphne was under a tree, fully dressed, hugging her knees. Laurel waited for her to say that they

75

both always got as red as lobsters, so why bother.

Silence.

It wasn't like her sister not to rise to the bait.

"Hey, what's wrong?" Laurel sat up. "What's the matter?"

Daphne shrugged, slightly, and said nothing.

And Laurel knew right then. She knew.

"Oh." She said it softly.

Daphne didn't cry, though she looked like she wanted to. She just sat, immobile. Not statue-immobile, but dead-fish-immobile, roadkill.

"But you love him," Laurel said. "So it's a wonderful thing. Right?"

"I guess so." Her voice was barely audible.

"Oh, come on, it's 1970, you lost your virginity, it's not like the old days. I can't believe you beat me to it. I'm the oldest! I'm supposed to go first!"

That worked. "For once!" Daphne laughed. "You don't think it's wrong?" she asked a minute later. Laurel thought, If you feel so awful, maybe I do think it's wrong, but she said, "Of course not. It's not the Middle Ages."

"I feel shitty, though. Why?"

"Because you're a big old slut with big

old privities!" Laurel said. That made Daphne laugh again, and they went inside to fix sandwiches for lunch. But Laurel thought, Yeah, why? Why do you feel shitty? She had slept with her boyfriend months ago. It was such a relief to get it over with. She hadn't told Daphne, and Daphne hadn't guessed. Because I didn't mope and posture like Sarah Bernhardt, Laurel thought.

"Your life is very dramatic," she said to Daphne.

Daphne sighed. Dramatically.

CITE´SS. *n.s.* [from *cit.*] A city woman. A word peculiar to *Dryden.*
— *A Dictionary of the English Language*
by Samuel Johnson

The twins went to separate colleges for their first year, but they found they did not like being in separate small liberal arts schools in small, icy communities, and they both transferred to Pomona, a small liberal arts school in a small, sunny community. After graduation, they hung around Los Angeles for a couple of years waitressing, then decided it was finally time to come home. They agreed that by "home" they did not mean Larchmont; they meant New York City, home to all.

They couldn't afford the West Village, and they wouldn't consider the Upper West Side, home of recently graduated Columbia students and the elderly. The Upper East Side was not even a passing thought. They had one friend who lived in the West Forties, an eccentric actress who spent all her time with drag queens. Otherwise, everyone they knew lived below Fourteenth Street.

But by the time they got to the last apartment of the day — "the dump finale," as Daphne put it — and hauled themselves up the four flights of stairs covered in worn green linoleum, the banister sturdy and thick with a century of layers of darker green paint, Laurel was longing to share a boxy postwar studio with ten stewardesses on York Avenue. The East Village was grimy and ominous. The apartments they'd seen were more grimy and more ominous still. She was so tired that the stairway they were on now seemed the grimiest and most ominous of all, though it wasn't, it was just green. Dogs barked from behind doors. A couple fought in Spanish. The smell of cooking here, the smell of wine there. The landlady had ankles as thick as tree trunks and wheezed on each landing as she led them skyward. Laurel thought of carrying groceries up the steps. What if you forgot toilet paper?

There were four locks on the door, one of them a long iron rod with one end fitted into a metal plate in the floor. On the windows were metal accordion fences, also locked. Outside, a rickety fire escape.

But beyond the fire escape, Laurel saw rooftops and the steeple of a church. There was a bleary skylight that probably leaked. Gray light filled the three little rooms. The church bells rang. The stove was so old it looked like something from a silent movie. Laurel breathed in the air that smelled empty and full, like dust and new paint.

"It's like a garret," she said. "In Paris."

"It *is* a garret," Daphne said.

Our very own garret, Laurel thought.

"Our very own garret," Daphne said.

Was there anyone who understood anyone else as well as she and Daphne understood each other? There was no need to explain or justify wanting to climb linoleum M. C. Escher stairs to live in a tenement their grandparents had probably moved out of the minute they could, because Daphne already understood. Understanding is love, Laurel thought. She put her arm around her sister.

"Aren't we lucky?" Daphne said. "Together in a garret."

They stood quietly enjoying the dim light of autumn through unwashed windows.

Whenever the wind blew outside, Laurel

and Daphne could hear it whistling — like a phantom looking for its phantom dog, Laurel said. They named the phantom dog Mariah.

You walked through the front door with all its rattling locks and bolts into a kitchen that also served as living and dining room. Their mother asked why they didn't share a bedroom and turn the second room into a living room.

"Why don't we just move into a studio and be done with it? Sleep in the same bed? Come on, Mom. We're twins, but we're not babies anymore."

They did end up curled side by side sometimes, asleep in one bed, especially when it was cold, but there was no need to tell their mother that.

They bought a cheap futon couch, painted a wooden crate white to use as a coffee table, and found a beautiful oak chair on the street. By the window, between the ancient stove and the half refrigerator, they squeezed a small table they found at an antique store on Fourth Avenue that, they suspected, sold castoffs from the Goodwill. At the actual Goodwill Daphne picked up another chair with a tall ladder back, a shredded rush seat, and a small combination lock forever attached to one of its rungs.

"I thought it important to accessorize," Daphne said, spinning the lock's dial fondly. "And maybe someday we'll figure out the combination."

"And free the chair."

"And it will turn into a prince."

"Two princes."

"Two princes. And they'll sit down on the futon and say, *Where's my breakfast, woman?* And we'll kick them down the stairs."

"And we'll have to buy a new chair."

Daphne stretched out to the extent possible on the futon and said, "Where's my breakfast, woman?"

Laurel made some coffee, the only thing she knew how to make. They drank silently, Daphne still on the futon, Laurel on the ornately carved wooden chair. They listened to the wind called Mariah, then the thump of large raindrops on the skylight, which, it turned out, did not leak at all.

Sally and Arthur came to the apartment just one time, an easy drive, the car redolent with roast chicken Sally was bringing for her daughters.

"Why do you have to live in such a dangerous neighborhood?" she asked them at the door. "It's a jungle. A concrete jungle."

"I forbid it," their father said. "I absolutely forbid it."

"Welcome. Come in and sit down," Daphne said.

Arthur and Sally sat with exaggerated discomfort on the futon. "You've already been robbed twice," Sally said. "What are you waiting for? Three's a charm?"

"They took a speaker, but they left the other. Would you like some music?"

"Oh for Pete's sake," Sally said.

"They couldn't carry everything," Laurel said.

"That's the upside of living on the fifth floor," said Daphne.

"And it keeps our weight down."

The girls put the chicken in the refrigerator and convinced their parents to return to the street to eat spicy scraps of someone else's chicken in a questionable sauce while out-of-season Christmas lights blinked around them. After the visit, during the exit of which a wino tried to wash their windshield with a filthy rag before collapsing facedown on the hood of the car, Sally decided she would not return.

"Never, never, never," she said as they waited for the drunken soul to roll off their car. "Never again."

"But we do have to keep checking on

them," Arthur said when they got home. "They live in Needle Park without the park."

She grunted her assent, then said, "But they are each other's keepers. I always feel that is true."

Arthur was unwrapping a new cylinder of Rolaids. Indian food did not agree with him. "I forbade it," he said. "I absolutely forbade it. You heard me."

Sometimes, when Sally thought of the two girls, she imagined two knights, each astride a muscled, prancing horse, each holding a lance, the lances crossed in solidarity. There was something chivalrous about the way the twins were with each other, she thought. "They'll look out for each other, Arthur."

"They live in a slum."

"Together."

Arthur said "Hellhole," threw some more Rolaids into his mouth, and got into bed. "I forbade it."

"Yes, you did," Sally said in a soothing voice. "Yes, you did."

All that remained missing from their lives as young New Yorkers was a job. Two jobs, ideally. For years, Laurel had secretly feared that she would end up supporting Daphne because Daphne refused to learn to type.

She could too easily picture them, two old twins, their red hair faded into a mélange of pink, beige, and gray, Laurel typing away to earn a meager living, Daphne sitting at home complaining.

Daphne used to watch Laurel practice her typing with affectionate pity, explaining that if you never learned this secretarial skill you could never be a secretary. Then she would sigh before turning back to whatever novel she was reading and murmur, "Oh, Laurel, what will we do with ourselves?"

Laurel wanted to say that she did not know what "we" would do, that they were not shackled together like runaway convicts from the chain gang.

But apparently she was wrong. For here she was, a temp typing words she did not even bother to read, while Daphne did not. What did Daphne do while Laurel was typing in one midtown office and then another? Daphne read the want ads looking for jobs that did not require typing.

Such jobs were scarce, Daphne discovered. And those few that did not require typing so often required something else she did not have, like a master's degree in economics.

So it was with great joy that Laurel waved her sister off to an interview for a receptionist job, no typing or advanced degree required, at the East Village's new alternative newspaper. *DownTown* was not as prestigious as *The Village Voice* or *The SoHo Weekly News,* but Daphne was willing to give it a try, she told her sister.

Laurel, who could see fear and trepidation in her sister's eyes, said, "Yes, see how you like the place. An interview is just an interview. No commitment." Daphne had never been one to rush into new situations. That had always been Laurel's task. She wished she could come with Daphne, push her through the door, cheer her on from the sidelines. But she could at least cheer her on from the garret.

"Very Mary Tyler Moore," she said.

"To be unmarried and thirty in Minneapolis — every girl's dream. I'll be sure to wear a beret," Daphne said, but she did seem cheered by the thought, and on the morning of the interview Laurel heard her singing the theme song in the shower.

The hallway leading to the paper's office was painted the yellow of old, urine-soaked newspaper. The top half of the door was mottled glass with the name DOWNTOWN on it in black letters. Daphne entered a room with an empty desk facing her. There was a telephone on it, a few chairs opposite it, and a closed door behind it. She sat down facing the empty desk, smiled at it in a way she hoped showed competence and intelligence, then sighed and slumped back and checked her watch. The interview was for eleven o'clock. It was 10:55.

The room was the same color as the hallway. It had a hollow, chalky smell, the smell of abandonment, like a classroom after school has let out. She half expected a bell to ring and children to rush past her swinging their lunch boxes. She heard voices from the other side of the door, angry voices. Were they yelling at the previous applicant? Was the previous applicant yelling back? It was 11:10 now. Had they forgotten her appointment?

There was a cigarette butt on the floor. She kicked it beneath her chair.

It was 11:30. She had skipped breakfast because she was nervous. She needed a cup of coffee. And the cigarette butt on the floor reminded her that she was desperate for a cigarette. She put her hand into her purse and fumbled around, her eyes on the door, until she found the pack. It was empty.

The phone on the desk rang. It rang and rang until Daphne could not stand it. She picked it up. *"DownTown,"* she said.

"I need to talk to Richard Fucking Goldstein."

"He doesn't fucking work here," she said. She pushed open the door and yelled, "Doesn't anyone answer the fucking phone around here?"

She was hired immediately. The last receptionist had quit after one of the writers punched him in the face for saying Charles Mingus was more important than Charlie Parker.

"You'll end up running the joint," Laurel said. "You'll see."

They were on their way back from a celebratory dinner of Mexican food and margaritas.

"Two incomes!" Daphne said. "We can have caviar tacos! Every night!"

"Every other night," Laurel said. "Because, you see, I quit my job today."

Daphne stopped and stared at her sister. Laurel looked away. Two thin young men shuffled past. They looked like winter saplings, she thought, sticks of skinny legs planted in big buckled boots.

"You what?"

Laurel watched a drunk weave his way toward them, zigzagging crazily from one side of the sidewalk to the other, his dog on its leash zigzagging patiently behind him.

"I quit," she said, sidestepping the drunk and his loyal dog.

"You can't do that," Daphne said. "Why would you quit? No, you can't, Laurel. *N-O.*"

"I quit because I hate it. You were right. I never should have learned to type."

"Oh my god, oh my god." Daphne was walking quickly now, her head bowed with worry. "It's too much responsibility."

"We'll be fine. I promise."

"What if I end up hating my job? And I quit? Then what? One of us has to earn some money. For god's sake, Laurel."

"I promise I'll get a new job, okay?" She said it in their private twin language, and Daphne calmed down.

The truth was, Laurel already had a new job. She'd gotten it even before she quit typing. She wouldn't start for a week, but for that week, she said nothing about it to her sister. When Daphne left for work in the morning, Laurel pretended to be asleep. When she returned, Laurel greeted her in a fog of marijuana smoke. She wasn't sure why she held back. Partly it was easier not to tell Daphne, who would be contemptuous of what she was embarking on, which was teaching, bad enough, but teaching kindergarten, even worse, and teaching kindergarten at a private school. *Private school!* Daphne would say. *The parents have to pay for teachers like you with no teaching credentials whatsoever? What a scam!*

Yes, there was the desire to put off her sister's scorn for as long as possible. But more than that, oh, so much more than that, Laurel had to admit, was the guilty but acute pleasure she took in watching Daphne squirm.

"I can't keep this boat afloat alone," Daphne kept saying. "Look at you! You're a complete degenerate."

This was not the first time Laurel had held things back from her sister. She could sometimes feel herself clutching at the details of her life, keeping them for herself as long as possible — just little things that happened, an observation, a passing sensation, which she did not want to let go of. She had never minded sharing toys or clothes or candy with her sister the way some children, children like Brian, minded. But she didn't want to share everything that befell her — or might befall her. She didn't want it all to disappear into her sister's existence. Was that selfish? The one person she might have asked was Daphne.

Sometimes Daphne and Laurel still dressed identically. It was not economical

— far better to swap clothes, effectively doubling their wardrobe. But Sally sometimes bought them matching jackets or scarves. She couldn't help herself. Today, they were wearing the leather jackets their mother had given them for their birthday. And white jeans. Their red hair was bright even in the city sun, and people they passed glanced at them, some smiling, some puzzled. A woman not much older than they were hurried on the sidewalk, hauling a recalcitrant little boy beside her. He stared openmouthed at them. Daphne stuck her tongue out at the boy, and he scuttled after his mother.

Laurel said, "Why would you do that to a child?"

"Why wouldn't you?"

They linked arms. The day was crisp, the limp city alive again, the summer smell of decay whisked away.

"I like your jacket," Laurel said.

"My mother gave it to me."

They went into a deli and ordered blintzes.

"Which is better, the way sour cream looks or tastes?" Daphne asked.

"Tie."

Daphne thought about that as they ate, looking at the beautiful, shimmering sour cream, tasting it cool and smooth against the warm, buttery blintz. Could anything really be a tie? Was anything really equal to any other thing? She and Laurel were twins, eggs of a feather, so to speak, but were they tied? Tied together, yes. But tied?

" 'Tie' is a funny word," she said.

"Sometimes," Laurel said, "I think all words are funny."

After a week of indolence, Laurel came home with a bag of new pencils and pens and an assignment book.

"What's all that for?"

"You may call me Miss Laurel from now on. I got a job as a kindergarten teacher at a private school on the Upper West Side."

Daphne gave her a sharp look. She hated her sister's secrets. "I hate this, Laurel. Why do you do this?"

"Look, I meant to tell you earlier, but somehow I didn't."

"Somehow? You sneaky snake of a sister. You're a teacher?"

"Oh, Daphne, I'm sorry I didn't tell you, it's just —"

But Daphne was raising her hand now, like a child in a classroom, waving it frantically. "Call on me, Miss Laurel! Call on *me*!"

"The school was desperate."

"They must have been." Daphne embraced her sister. "Miss Laurel, Miss Laurel! You need a bell. They'll love you. You'll be like Miss Crabtree in *The Little Rascals*. They'll all have a crush on you. And then midgets will sneak into the class, but I can't remember why, can you? Oh god, I'm so relieved."

"No, really, they were so desperate they went to the temp agency, then they asked me in for the interview two weeks ago — that's only two weeks before school starts. I wonder what happened."

"Someone must have had a nervous breakdown. Or gone to jail."

"Or gotten pregnant."

"Don't get pregnant, Miss Laurel. Just don't. We can't afford another mouth to feed."

Funny to think of her sister as a teacher. Teachers were so old. Daphne thought of Mrs. Piper, the oldest teacher at their high school, who taught Latin and wore her hair in a bun. One day, it must have been the first day of sophomore year, when she and Laurel switched from Spanish to Latin, the twins wore their father's pajama tops to school to protest something having to do with the dress code, she could no longer remember what. They had expected a proper pedantic scolding and a trip to the principal's office from Mrs. Piper, who was famously strict. Instead, she seemed not to notice the large long-sleeved pajama tops. She clapped her hands with pleasure at their first names, their last name, and their twinship.

"Daphne, the goddess who turned into a *laurel* tree! And Wolfe," she said, smiling at them. She read to them from Plutarch — the story of Romulus and Remus — in Latin, then translated. When she read aloud, " 'We are told that they were named from 'ruma,' the Latin word for *teat,* because they were seen sucking the wild beast,' " the class began to snicker, and she clapped her hands again and said, " *'Nam risu inepto res ineptior nulla est!'* There is nothing more foolish than a foolish laugh! Catullus, canto thirty-nine. But no more Catullus, *discipuli,* until you have matured."

Of course, the twins went to the library immediately after class to look up Catullus, number thirty-nine. They knew a challenge when they heard one. It was a poem making fun of a man with a big shiny smile. Catullus said he obviously brushed his teeth with urine.

Laurel stood at the sink, getting ready for her first day of teaching, brushing her teeth with Colgate.

"Remember Mrs. Piper? Our first class?" Daphne said. "I wonder if any of your students will be wearing their father's pajama tops."

"Oh, I forgot about that!"

"Oh."

"I do remember Catullus," Laurel said. "And the man polishing his teeth with piss. I could read Catullus to the children! They would love me forever."

Daphne laughed. Anyway, why should her sister remember the pajama tops? "I'll walk you to the subway."

They were on the street in front of their building. An abandoned armchair leaned against a metal pole with a bent metal sign that, Daphne knew, had parking regulations printed on it. But it was unreadable now, folded in on itself like a closed book. Daphne took her sister's arm and they set off in the warm, cloying drizzle. She could feel Laurel's nervousness.

"They're just little kids," she said. "You can tell them anything. Like Brian!"

"Children, a freak of nature is a princess who can fly."

"A princess who could fly would be a freak of nature, so . . ."

At the top of the subway stairs, Daphne

95

called, "Goodbye! Good luck!" in their private language, waving encouragement.

A man pushed past her muttering "Foreigners."

Laurel had chosen a tweed skirt and a silk blouse, and she hoped she looked teacherly. It was her only suitable outfit, but absolutely unsuitable for the unseasonably hot, rainy day. The subway steamed with damp people on their way to work. A woman passed her a laminated card that said I AM DEAF PLEASE HELP BUY, and offered her a green plastic key chain in the shape of a seahorse. When the businessmen with polished shoes got off at Fifty-Seventh Street, Laurel was finally able to find a seat.

She didn't particularly want to be a teacher. She didn't want to be anything. She wanted to read books and go jogging past the garbage along the river.

The floor of the subway car was smeared with street dirt and rain. Her shoes were suede, now spotted with rain, smart choice, Laurel. And she had no boyfriend. And she was a schoolteacher. A spinster school-teacher.

"The class size is manageable," the head-master had said at the interview. He was the most frazzled person Laurel had ever seen.

One of his pockets was inside out. His hair was limp and clammy with sweat, and it was thinning in odd places, like a neglected lawn. "Fifteen children," he said. He blinked at her hopefully.

"Oh yes, perfectly manageable," she said. Fifteen children? She tried to imagine fifteen children in a room, but could picture only a blurry, amalgamated sort of mob of small moving figures.

"The curriculum is quite basic," the headmaster continued, "so your major in psychology won't come into play too much, although it certainly can't hurt."

Laurel had majored in classics, but she'd seen no reason to argue. The poor man clearly had enough troubles. She was tempted to look in her purse and find a comb for him. Or a tissue. Spare change. A cracker.

Mr. Gravit handed her a grubby manila folder stuffed with mimeographed sheets of paper. "Will this help? It's just kindergarten, after all. I'm sure you'll do fine."

"Oh yes," Laurel said. "I spent last summer working at a kennel, you know."

"Yes," said the headmaster, ushering her out the door. "I saw that on your résumé. Very apt. Very apt."

In the two weeks since the interview,

Laurel had studied the mimeographed sheets, but they didn't give her much assistance. The letter *B* followed by broken lines beside a drawing of a beach ball, that kind of thing. The words to "Ring Around the Rosie," which she thought most people, including the children, must already know by heart. A lesson plan for gluing macaroni onto oaktag paper. She had a box of macaroni in her bag that first morning, hoping the oaktag would be in the classroom.

By the time Laurel climbed the subway steps at Eighty-Sixth and Central Park West, it was pouring. She opened an umbrella she'd brought with her, but it was not terribly effective, and both shoulders and arms were soaked by the time she arrived at school. She climbed the steps, so wide and impressive they could have led to a museum; an unimportant museum, admittedly; a museum of, say, philology. She was early, and the halls were almost empty. She went down a narrow, dank stairway that she thought she remembered led to an adult ladies' room and pushed open a heavy wooden door on which was taped a sheet of construction paper with the word LADY'S scrawled in red crayon. Belonging to just one lady, she thought. Should she correct the sign? It seemed too aggressive an act for her first day teaching kindergarten. She put on lipstick at the mirror in the fluorescent light. She missed Daphne. She tried to pat her shirt dry with a rough paper towel. Then she went back up the stairway, her sleeves clinging.

Shivering within the wet, cold silk of her blouse, she tried to focus on the children. She tried not to favor the attractive ones, of which there were four. The rest were a blur of garments appliquéd with zoo animals. And one little girl with an enormous eagle's nest of curly black hair who frequently crossed her arms in obvious disapproval of the new teacher.

"The most important thing," Laurel said, "is not to be afraid of making mistakes. Making a mistake is how you learn what's right."

The little girl with the hair that surely harbored a large bird of prey gave her an astonished look. It was not a look of astonished liberation, as Laurel momentarily hoped. It was a look of astonished pity. *You blundering amateur,* said the look. The child actually rolled her eyes.

Laurel looked away, pulled at her wet silk sleeve. She watched it peel off her arm, translucent, just like the peeling skin of sunburns long ago.

■ ■ ■ ■

If Laurel was a teacher, Daphne wondered why she, Daphne, was a receptionist rather than, say, a recepter. If a teacher teaches, does a receptionist-recepter recept? While Laurel tried to ambush fifteen children and cajole them into sitting cross-legged on the floor, Daphne sat at the desk in the vestibule of the alternative weekly trying to think up a better name for what she did, which was, alas, she thought, nothing.

Her tenure was certainly less exciting than the tales about her predecessor had promised: there were no fistfights, and the staff did not trust her enough as the new person to handle their drug transactions. In fact, she seemed to be invisible to everyone there.

Sometimes she left the office early, and no one appeared to care or even notice. Laurel was done teaching by 2:30, and they liked to meet at a large old coffeehouse on Greenwich, drink iced cappuccinos, and complain about their jobs. The chairs at the café had twisted wire legs and twisted wire backs. It was warm and dim, and the walls were lined with enormous dusty old oil paintings. Classical music played, the espresso machines hissed, and an immense statue of Pan playing his pipes looked down at them. The smell of coffee was sweet and rich and dreamy.

"I just leave the door to the office open, and no one has to bother me going in or out," she told Laurel at one of these drowsy coffee dates. "I mean, once I figured out how to route phone calls to the right person, there's just about nothing for me to do. It's very boring. But I can't completely relax because there is always the little, teeny, tiny possibility someone will ask me something, though I can't imagine who or for what, but it is a job and they do pay me, but it means I can't completely concentrate on what I'm reading. And if you are not concentrating on Henry James, you're in trouble."

"You're reading *Washington Square,* not *The Wings of the Dove.*"

"You try it. Looking over your shoulder all the time, just in case. It's very distracting."

Laurel gave her a pitying look. "I have read nothing but dinosaur books since I started. I don't have time to look over my shoulder. I feel like a mechanical rabbit on the greyhound track. Also, do you know how many times we've listened to *Free to Be . . . You and Me?*"

Daphne said, "Mel Brooks! Carol Channing!"

"It still gets their attention. But the record only lasts forty-six minutes."

"Read them *Washington Square*. I'll audit the class."

"We started singing all our lessons. Even art projects, which is practically all we do. Glue and sing. Sing and glue."

"It sounds idyllic," Daphne said.

"They're like little animals with opposable thumbs. But it has its pleasures. I can't imagine having the freedom to read a real book, though."

They looked at each other, both suddenly grinning.

"Yes?" Daphne asked.

"Yes!" Laurel answered.

To Swop. *v.a.* [Of uncertain derivation.] To change; to exchange one thing for another. A low word.

— *A Dictionary of the English Language*
by Samuel Johnson

What was the point of being a twin if you couldn't pull the old switcheroo? At her sister's receptionist desk in the vestibule outside *DownTown,* Laurel sat properly, facing front, not reading, trying to enjoy the switcheroo but finding it tedious. Daphne, she had to admit, was right: the job was to sit at the desk and answer the phone and announce anyone who came in, but the phone did not ring and no one arrived needing or wanting to be announced.

Laurel peeked into the main office. No one looked up. She pretended she belonged there and began to weave her way through the desks and cubbyhole cubicles, marveling at the shabbiness of the place. Despite everything Daphne had told her, she had expected something more glamorous, but all she saw were menacing, leaning piles of newspapers lining the walls; small desks suffering beneath large typewriters, telephones, dirty mugs, and heaping ashtrays. Rolling chairs were frozen in place by the miserably curved backs and tapping feet of their occupants. In an aquarium-like glassed-in enclosure, a tall woman and a short man shook their fists at each other, silent behind the glass, like exotic fighting fish.

Laurel stopped at a table of open dictionaries and style guides. At last, something worth looking at. Glancing down at a smeary sheet of galleys over which a woman with dirty black hair was hunched, she said, " 'Callous.' With an *o.* "

"Oh god," the woman said. "That's embarrassing. 'The callus behavior of the Koch administration . . .' I wonder how a callus would behave."

"Callously."

The woman laughed and introduced herself as Becky. Laurel remembered she was supposed to be Daphne just in time, introduced herself as her sister, and said, "You get to correct everyone's homework?"

"Yup. I'm the exalted copy chief."

"My dream job."

Becky snorted. "Right."

"No? I think it would be fun. Better than sitting at the front desk staring at the dirty wall."

By the time she went back to her post, Laurel had a pile of pages to read and copy-edit. It was just a trial, Becky said. She already used four or five freelancers. But maybe some work would pop up for Laurel, whom she called Daphne, if she did a good job.

As she made her way to meet Daphne, Laurel thought she had already done an excellent job. Daphne would be so pleased. No one had missed the real Daphne and, better yet, the impostor Daphne had impressed the powers that be to promote (probably) the real Daphne.

When Laurel arrived, triumphant, at the café, her sister was not yet there. Laurel hoped the children hadn't locked Daphne in the coat closet or something. She ordered a cannoli while she waited, then another to celebrate her success, then a cappuccino to wash it down. Sated and rather sleepy, she thought: I pulled it off; more than pulled it off, I've given Daphne's career a boost. A little guiltily, she wondered how Daphne had fared. Daphne was not a forceful person in new situations. If she had been, she would have discovered Becky and the copy desk herself. Laurel, exhilarated by her own success, suffered a pang of guilt at the thought of Daphne, an innocent, surrounded by so many small, sweet savages.

Daphne had, herself, felt reservations on her way to Laurel's classroom that morning, reservations she had not shared with her sister. It was her idea to switch jobs, after all, unless it had been Laurel's — it was often hard to tell — but either way she had enthusiastically gone along with the plan. As she stood at the bottom of the wide steps leading up to the school, though, she was no longer enthusiastic. She was terrified. The children would eat her alive and pick the bones clean. They would dance over the carcass of the fraudulent Miss Wolfe, banging wooden blocks together and dinging on their triangles or whatever musical instruments children in kindergarten had these days. Did they really call Laurel Miss Laurel? Or did they call her Miss Wolfe? It was an exclusive private school, after all. But they would taunt her by whatever name they chose and use their crayons and markers to write graffiti on the walls, on the windows. Then they would throw each other out the windows. Then they would throw her out the window. Could they reach the windows?

The headmaster stood at the top of the steps greeting his employees. When Daphne reached him, he did not narrow his eyes or ask to see her passport. He shook her hand and said good morning. She recognized him from her sister's description.

"Sir," she said politely. "Your sweater is on inside out. And backwards."

"Is it?" He smoothed the sweater affectionately. "Perhaps I put it on that way at home."

"Would you like me to hold your clipboard while you fix it?"

Mr. Gravit pondered her offer. "No," he said at last. "Thank you, Miss Wolfe. What's done is done."

Miss Wolfe. Yes, she was Miss Wolfe. She was not claiming to be anyone else. She tried to relax.

The children entered the classroom in little bursts of energy, shyness, petulance, joy. They were so small. If they attacked, she was sure she could fend them off. She began to feel more confident. When there were fifteen of them, Daphne sang the

107

alphabet and some simple spelling words with them. They sang with enthusiasm. They did everything with enthusiasm, even refusing to sit down. Were they noticing anything different about their teacher? She hoped not. They were so amusing, crawling over each other, chewing on cardboard cutouts of numbers.

As the day went on, she noticed one child in particular eyeing her suspiciously, a girl with wild hair and a sequined band around her head.

"Something the matter?" Daphne asked. What was the little girl's name? Daphne had no idea. "Dear?" she added.

The child put her small hands on her small hips, leaned her face and the full force of her gigantic hair forward, and stared. Daphne stared back. She was sure the child had figured out she was not the real Laurel. They could tell — she knew it; she should never have participated in this needless charade. They had instincts. They could smell it. They could smell fear, and they could smell an impostor. They were like dogs. You could not trick a dog.

Finally the girl said, "Sdack."

Daphne said, "Sdack?" Was that a taunt? A kindergarten curse? Did this class have its own secret language?

"Sdack!" the girl said, her eyes bugging out, her little foot stamping the floor.

"Snack! Snack!" they all began yelling. "You forgot snack!"

"Oh! Snack!" Daphne smiled. "I am so sorry, children. So I did." She handed out their graham crackers and milk cartons.

"Would you like to be my assistant?" she asked the little girl with the hair and sequins, who continued periodically to shoot her the evil eye. Daphne thought, Keep your enemies close. She said, "You never know, I might forget something else. As my assistant, you can keep me on the straight and narrow."

The child glared at her, then said in her nasal voice, "Yedth, all wight." And she did assist. She was officious and condescending — a perfect assistant, really. When it was time to go, she ran up to Daphne and hugged her.

"You have tamed the wee serpent," Mr. Gravit said from the doorway after the girl had run past him with a slap on his knee from her fat little hand.

"She certainly helped me out today," Daphne said. She still did not know the girl's name. All day she had been addressing the child as Assistant.

"Miranda's a somewhat forceful child,"

the headmaster said. "Bit of a pain in the ass, actually."

"Oh no, I wouldn't say that."

"No, you wouldn't. You mustn't. But I would. She is my daughter, after all."

Her gaudy outfit made more sense now.

"Spoiled, demanding . . ." the headmaster was saying, a whole list of unpleasant qualities, in a sort of singsong.

"Good for her," Daphne said. "How else does anyone get anything?"

Mr. Gravit nodded. "You understand children very well, Miss Wolfe. Well, I'm glad she was of use. She is the light of my life."

When Daphne at last made her entrance into the café, it was exactly that: an entrance. She swept the door open, swooped into the room, stretched her arms, and aimed herself like a big redheaded bird at her sister. "I did it, I did it," she sang to the tune of "You Did It" from *My Fair Lady.* "You said that I would do it, and indeed I did."

Laurel listened as Daphne recounted her conquest of the kindergarten class. Her fears were unfounded, it appeared. Daphne had even made headway with Miranda Gravit.

"This is amazing!" she said. "You're a better me than I am."

But I'm a better you than you are, she added silently. And she proceeded to tell Daphne how she had impersonated her into a new job as a copy editor.

Daphne, still jubilant from her successful day as her sister, could not take it in at first. "Becky?" She tried to picture Becky but could only call up a murky image of a nondescript person in a mustard-colored sweater. "Really? Me?"

"This one writer wrote 'one of the only' and I changed it to 'one of the few,' " Laurel said. "I think that's why we got the job."

"Thank you," Daphne said. "I can't believe it. Thank you!" She wondered if she would have noticed "one of the only." Of course she would have. She wondered why she had never noticed Becky. She wondered why Becky had never noticed her.

"Well, congratulations on a job well done," she said, a tiny bit deflated somehow, as if neither success was really success at all. "Nobody missed me!"

"Or me!"

"We said that we would do it . . ."

"And indeed we did."

The sisters sat quietly for a moment. Outside, a sheet of dirty newspaper blew

111

past the windows.

"The Assistant was wearing a crown as well as a headband," Daphne said at last. "I didn't see it at first."

"It was lurking in her Garfunkel hair? She's a difficult little girl. But sometimes I catch her staring at nothing, daydreaming, and I think what an interesting adult she will probably turn out to be."

"You're such an optimist, Laurel."

"Everyone needs a hobby."

"Everything about poor Mr. Gravit is askew, isn't it?"

"He looks like someone left him in the dryer," said Laurel.

"A forgotten sock."

That night, Daphne began to work on the galley Laurel had brought home, a review of a play. "It's a play about a consciousness-raising session," she said. "The audience joins in. Isn't that a little passé?"

"Luckily, you don't have to see the lousy play. Just help the words sort themselves out. And be glad you're not a teacher."

"These words are just as confused and squirmy as children."

They both looked affectionately at the galley.

"But they don't hug," Daphne added.

"But they have to be listened to, just like

children."

Words and students, Laurel thought — they could be recalcitrant, out of order, trying to slip by without being noticed. But once you got them working together, unobtrusive and efficient, it was beautiful.

"Of course, words never have to go to the bathroom, and you don't have to wipe their noses," Daphne said. "I still can't understand why *I* never noticed Becky and the wonderful world of copyediting."

"You don't notice anybody. You have your nose in a book, as they say."

"Laurel, you're not really going to fix your nose, are you?"

Laurel shrugged, looked away, stood up. "I might," she said. "Why shouldn't I?"

"Because . . ."

"Why shouldn't I if I want to?"

"Because . . ."

"We're not a two-headed monster, Daphne."

"Hey, I'm not the one planning to disfigure myself."

"Plastic surgery is not disfigurement. And I'm not planning to tamper with your nose, so lay off."

Then we won't be interchangeable, Daphne thought sadly.

"We're not interchangeable," Laurel

added, as if she'd heard her sister's thoughts.

Daphne wanted a boyfriend. The feeling was one not just of desire but of deficiency. She felt inadequate not having a boyfriend: incomplete. She believed that being a twin sister and having a twin sister was a kind of magic circle that would always protect her from being alone, yet she felt alone. A terrible admission. How disloyal she was. And childish, as if she could not manage on her own. She didn't manage on her own, didn't have to: Laurel was there, her older sister, her alter ego, on whom she had always been able to rely. She knew that Laurel would always be there. But what if she wasn't?

Anyway, there it was, the sad truth: She wanted a boyfriend.

She wanted someone by her side, on her side, a man, not her sister. Or not just her sister.

She wondered if the closeness between Laurel and her seemed outlandish to the outside world. It sometimes seemed outlandish to her. Most people probably thought it was part of being an identical twin. And that was true, she knew that was true, she could feel the connection to Laurel in her cells. But all the same, it was peculiar to be so close to someone who was not a boyfriend. Or a husband.

A husband. Because that was what she really wanted, wasn't it? A husband. She could not admit it to anyone, not even Laurel, least of all Laurel. She would sound like someone out of the 1950s. She might as well start wearing a little hat and gloves. But she did, she wanted a husband, a person to sink into, to rely on, to sleep with every night, to have sex with every night, to wake up with every morning. To love.

Was that too much to ask?

She was lucky, she thought, that her job served as a surrogate boyfriend. Her job now was demanding and capricious, jealous of her time and filling up her inner life with its needs and moods.

"There are rhythms," she told Laurel. "It's uneven, raggedy, like the breathing of someone who just ran up a hill. One minute a fact-checker is crying and the layout guy is on the roof getting high and the reporter you're working with starts yelling that he doesn't care if his participles dangle, and then the proofreader corrects the spelling of 'Cincinnati' to 'Cinncinatti,' and then, suddenly, just like that, the noise stops. The commotion stops. And you can go back to the quiet, precise, orderly routine of reading line by line, word by word." Her eyes were alive, her lips in a half smile. "I love my work."

"There is something fair and just in what we do," she said to Becky one day. "Grammar is good. I mean ethically good. If you think of all these words just staggering around, grammar is their social order, their government."

Becky, her face drawn and sallow, her cheek smudged with ink, put a cigarette in her mouth but did not light it. "I'll never quit smoking," she said. "How do people quit?"

Daphne said, "Grammar makes you respect words, every individual word. You make sure it's in the place where it feels the most comfortable and does its job best."

Becky flicked her lighter. "Mm-hmm." Slowly, she let the flame touch the end of the cigarette. Slowly, she inhaled. "You can't quit, just so you know. It's a myth."

"Every part of speech is as deserving as every other part of speech."

"Mmm," Becky said, with great satisfaction, smoke dribbling from the sides of her mouth. "Yes, it is. It's in the Constitution, I believe."

"Sometimes, okay, a word needs to be led. Or nudged. Or dragged. Or squeezed a little. To get it to the spot where it belongs."

"Or cut."

Daphne said, "Well, last resort."

"Different styles, you and I," Becky said.

Daphne thought, Yes, thank god for that. Becky was wearing the same old pilled sweater the color of expensive mustard, which smelled faintly of mothballs.

Becky tapped the manuscript she was reading. " 'I came home to him stumbling, peeing, and hiding,' " she read. "Now, which one would you say is stumbling, peeing, and hiding? The guy who came home to the junkie in his house, or the junkie? Then he writes, 'I gave him a bath in my shower with most of my clothes.' Do you think he means most of his clothes were in the bath sloshing around with the junkie? I mean, come on, people."

"But the point is, any collection of words can be copyedited with pleasure. Even this wash-the-junkie-intruder crap. Because we are bringing order to the world of wash-the-junkie-intruder crap. This is the best job I've ever had. Thank you, Becky."

"You're welcome," Becky said. "Personally, I'd rather get laid."

Yes, well, there was that. When she got home that evening, Daphne put on her pajamas and settled in for a good sulk. She had found, at the last minute, a "masterful" that should have been a "masterly," and she had inserted a semicolon in front of a conjunctive adverb. She had changed a "knelt" to a "kneeled," then changed it back again. She was good at her work. So what? It was Monday, the big night of the week, the paper rushing to its inevitably late close, and Daphne would have to go back in a few hours, but in the meantime she could stare into space and think about not having a boyfriend.

"Why are you home?" Laurel said when she came in. "Isn't this free-food night?"

"Yes."

Food was brought in every Monday night and served to the staff in great aluminum foil troughs.

"So? What's the story?"

"No story."

"Want me to come with you, the secret twin, and we can be at two ends of the room at once and freak people out?"

Daphne hated the word "freak." Even in ninth grade when all the kids they hung out with, the hippie kids who were not quite old enough to run away, called themselves freaks, Daphne had not liked the term.

"Oh come on, 'freak' means *capricious,*"

Laurel said. "*Whimsical*. At least, 'freak' *used* to mean *capricious* and *whimsical,* which is good enough for me."

"Well, I don't want to be capricious."

"Too bad."

Daphne said, "Whimsical would be okay."

"No."

"No."

Laurel looked at her sister, wasting away on a saggy futon, already in her pajamas, her expression woebegone, her hair up in an ugly tight bun, and said, "Yes, you are. You are whimsical. You're the most whimsical person in the world."

They both started to laugh.

"What's wrong?" Laurel asked. "Really, Daphne. What is it?"

Daphne hesitated and then said, very softly, a tremor in her voice, "Will I ever find a boyfriend?"

Laurel pushed her sister's feet out of the way and sat on the futon.

"Silly," she said. "You'll find a million boyfriends."

"I don't want a million boyfriends. I want one. A real one."

She had managed to assume a dramatic pose, even on the cramped futon, one arm flung across her face, the other falling languidly to the floor. But Laurel could sense the real fear and loneliness, the panic, almost. She recognized it because she so often felt it herself.

Of course Daphne would find a boyfriend, she told her. Daphne was a remarkable creature. She just needed a creature as remarkable as she was to be her remarkable boyfriend. She just needed to find the right one, one good enough and freaky enough and whimsical enough for her. "Come on, get dressed, we'll go freeload and find freeloader boyfriends. Up you go!"

They stood in line, then loaded their paper plates with yellow rice and greasy chicken wings.

"You're twins?" asked a young reporter who was just behind them.

"No," one of them said with a smile.

"Uh-uh," the other said, shaking her head.

They were wearing identical clothes — they had not been able to resist — plaid Kenzo dresses, courtesy of their mother.

One of the other star reporters came over, an Englishman, thin and wiry in a Mick Jagger sort of way. His suit was the color of good vanilla ice cream and he wore a short paisley silk scarf tied around his neck. A suit! *A neckerchief!* both girls were thinking. Older, in his thirties, he reeked of superiority; it was in his accent, in his walk, a bandy rock 'n' roll walk, in his vanilla-colored suit among the blue jeans and work shirts. He was charming, too, which was unfair, Daphne thought, like his work — eloquent, funny, rather brilliant, rather unfair. Did they all look like the stories they wrote? The way people look like their dogs?

"Well, well, well," said Jon the Englishman. "What have we here?"

"Diplopia," Laurel said, holding out her hand to shake his.

"Ibid," Daphne said, doing the same.

They smiled so openly when they spoke. It was a routine they had developed, and they relished, every time, that delicious moment, half a moment, quarter of a nanosecond, when they were believed, when whoever they were speaking to thought, Here are two girls named Diplopia and Ibid.

No wonder I don't have a boyfriend, Daphne thought in a flash. Then pushed it out of her head. She wondered if it would be unprofessional to sleep with Jon. She liked older men. She liked men who looked like dandies but were known to be philandering heels.

No wonder I don't have a boyfriend, she thought again.

That night, in Jon's rather squalid unmade

bed, she decided she had been right and wrong. She was right, it was unprofessional; and she was wrong, she did not like older men who were philandering heels all that much. Too smooth. Chest too smooth, words too smooth, sex too smooth.

"I have a question," he said, lying back against a slightly yellow pillow. "About you and your sister."

"No," she said immediately. "We never have. And, no, we don't want to."

He exhaled a cloud of smoke and a sound of mild disappointment.

"Not one of my personal fantasies, mind you," he said.

"One of your impersonal ones? What are your fantasies?"

"You really don't want to know, you sweet little girl."

She laughed, because he was right. "No, I don't."

"And now," he said, "what you do probably want to know is how I can help you leave behind the dreary confines of the copy desk for the glories of a byline." He crossed his white weedy arms over his white weedy chest. He flicked back his hair, which was thin, shiny, the color of golden wheat blown by a fresh, hushed breeze. His cigarette hung from his lips.

Daphne took a cigarette from his pack, unfiltered, ugh, but hers were in her bag in the living room and she was too comfortable to get up.

"You are very attractive," she said. "I don't know why."

"The first thing you need is a beat," he said. "A reporter needs a beat."

"But I don't want to be a reporter."

"Of course you do. You all do."

Daphne watched him pour more scotch into a glass and wished she liked scotch. "I don't," she said. "Reporters have to talk to people and ask them questions."

"How else do you discover the truth?"

"That's lofty. The truth! I guess I could read your column to find the truth, for starters. Because even though it's usually *not* true, it is very entertaining. And I've noticed you are not intimidated by the split infinitive. Is that because you're English?"

He took another swig of whiskey. "Yes," he said. "Privilege of lost empire." Then he grabbed her and brought his face close to hers. "And I think, young copy girl," he said, his breath warm and sweet with whiskey, "that it is time to split infinitives once more."

After another round of pleasant copulation, as Jon put it, Daphne declined his offer to spend the night, put her clothes on, and walked home in the humid springtime dark. It had been raining, and the sidewalks seemed to steam damp gray night air. She could hear her own footsteps. It was as if they were following her. She glanced back to make sure no one real was following, but the gay men strolling past were not interested in her. Neither were the drunks farther east.

She wondered if she would ever find someone she cared about. It was so draining, worrying about finding love, as if it were an upcoming exam. She liked sleeping with guys, liked the flirtation and the buildup, the funny, awkward dance that led at last to bed. Why was everyone, herself included, so determined to have a proper boyfriend? Everyone wants to be loved; everyone wants someone to love: that was the reason, obvious and bland and thrilling and eternal. God, it would be so nice, so restful, to call off the search.

Laurel watched her sister leave with the bandy-legged English reporter, sighed, then watched a man with shoulder-length hair and a large bald spot empty other people's chicken bones into a bag. "For soup," he happily explained to anyone who asked.

Laurel walked up to the roof to get some air. Too many adults were alarming. Children had the excuse of being children. But these people . . .

"These people?" a voice said. "Which people?"

She must have said it aloud. How much of her little homily, she wondered, had she spoken out loud?

"Those people," she said. "Any people. Too many people, that's all I meant. In one place."

"Eating."

"Talking."

He nodded. He seemed, in the dark of the rooftop, to be extremely good-looking.

"Why are you up here?" she asked.

"I live here. You?"

"Those people."

"Right."

They walked down the stairs to the street and into the bar next door. A jazz trio was playing, bass, piano, and horn.

"I live two floors above the paper," said the man, who was extremely good-looking even off the dark rooftop. His name was Larry. "I hate Monday nights."

"I don't even work there. My sister does. I was freeloading. But free food has its price. There was a man collecting old chewed chicken bones for soup."

Larry ordered them both cheeseburgers.

"Beer?"

"Beer," Laurel said.

She thought, I wonder if he would be a good boyfriend for Daphne? Then she thought, I wonder if he would be a good boyfriend for me?

EDA´CIOUS. *adj.* [*edax*, Latin.] Eating; voracious; devouring; predatory; ravenous; rapacious; greedy.
— *A Dictionary of the English Language*
by Samuel Johnson

When Laurel and Daphne first moved into the garret, they'd laughed about its ancient stove. They considered it decorative, like something from a stage set. They were afraid to light the burners and never had any reason to; they got every meal from the lunch counter on the corner, even breakfast, for which they ordered oatmeal that was slopped into a paper coffee cup decorated with Greek pillars. The kitchen with its half refrigerator, scratched sink, old stove, and cockroaches was not an inviting place to cook. And neither of them knew how.

Then Laurel suddenly — and stealthily, in Daphne's opinion — decided to learn. She

127

went on the hunt at secondhand bookstores for cookbooks. She called their mother and asked about recipes. Astonished when Sally explained the right way to cut a mushroom, Laurel realized she had never eaten a fresh mushroom, much less sliced one.

"I am embarking on an awed journey into the unknown."

She held the mushroom reverently in her hand. It was so light, so smooth, so dirty, and yet so otherworldly. It was like dead flesh. It was like fresh air.

She called her mother again. "Do you boil the water before you put the potato in or after?"

"Oh for god's sake, who eats boiled potatoes?" Daphne muttered.

"I hear you, Daphne, and I'm going to mash them, and you have to boil them before you mash them. Right, Mom?"

Sally said yes, you couldn't mash raw potatoes, and even Daphne should know that, and she was sorry she had failed them as a mother.

"She's sorry she failed us as a mother because you think mashed potatoes are raw," Laurel said to Daphne.

Their mother was in labor for twelve hours before the twins were born. Two nurses sat outside her hospital room playing cards. That was all Sally told them, except for how happy she had been.

"And I was a surprise!" Daphne would say when she was little.

"You're still a surprise," her mother would say, pulling her little body closer, kissing her forehead. But she had not been a surprise at all when she was born. Her parents had expected twins. Daphne understood that later: She was not the startling bonus, the icing on the cake, the cherry on top. She was the second child.

Daphne wondered what life had been like for the two of them in that womb. Did they fight over scarce resources? Did they elbow each other out of the way, once they had elbows? Did they tenderly bump and find comfort in the other little thing that resembled a shrimp, then a dolphin, an identical dolphin? Something must have happened between them in those nine months. You can't share a gestational sac for all that time without something going on.

An egg splits into two eggs. Somehow, one becomes two, not by adding another but by separating. Two halves become two wholes. Daphne reflected on that when she was young. The logic was both elusive and obvious. Eggs were such lovely things, their shape, the smooth, cool shells that held so much in their perfect, fragile grip. Laurel, unlike her sister, had been afraid of eggs. She'd read that eggs sometimes have double yolks. Double yolks mean double embryos. Double embryos take up double the space inside the egg. There isn't enough oxygen in the egg for both embryos. Usually, Laurel explained to anyone cooking or eating an egg, one of the embryos dies. Then it rots. It pollutes the egg environment. And then the other embryo dies. Laurel refused to acknowledge the difference between a fertilized and an unfertilized egg. Her sister ate eggs with abandon, said she felt an affinity for them. But for Laurel, the sight of a raw egg in a bowl had always made her queasy, the yolk quivering, a globe of coagulated yellow in trembling jellyfish-white.

Now she stood in the East Village kitchen cracking a brown-shelled egg into a glass bowl. Daphne stood in the doorway, dropped her bag and her coat onto the floor, and opened her mouth in pantomime astonishment. "Eggs? I can't believe what I'm seeing."

Laurel cracked another egg into a bowl.

"Is this some kind of aversion therapy?"

Laurel wondered if she could split the yolk in two and turn it into a double embryo.

She gingerly pulled the fork through the yolk. Of course the yolk broke. Egg whites were used as glue, weren't they? She tapped on the jellied substance. Or was it paint? Or was that eggshells? Or was that a color of paint? "I'm practicing," she said. "For when I have a boyfriend."

She broke another egg into the bowl, then another, and whipped them up with milk, salt, and pepper. She cooked them slowly, stirring them with a wooden spoon. They were a beautiful color. They were fluffy. She had made them herself.

"You will have to eat them, though," she said. "One can go only so far for love."

This was around the time Larry entered the picture.

"It's the cooking," she said to her sister. "It's like pheromones."

"Have you cooked anything for him yet?"

"No, but I think he can see it in my eyes."

"The pheromones or the scrambled eggs?"

"The womanly confidence and skills." And she started to laugh. "Oh! I make myself laugh!" she said through tears of laughter. "Oh god, I'm funny."

Daphne was not laughing. "How did you find a boyfriend at my place of business and I did not?"

"Why did you go home with an old poseur

and not up to the roof like me?"

Daphne had no answer. She knew that Laurel never would have gone home with Jon, though she didn't know why not, and that she would never have gone up to the roof alone at night, or anytime. It never would have occurred to her. Who wanders up to the rooftops of buildings? She had never even thought of the building as having a roof.

"He's not that old," she said. "I guess there's no one for me to meet at your place of business. Even on the roof."

"There's a sandbox on the roof."

"Is it Jewish?"

Laurel served her the scrambled eggs, which were surprisingly good.

Laurel had stayed at Larry's apartment a few times. It was enormous, almost empty of furniture, drafty, and had amazing views over the brownstones to the west.

"It used to be a showroom. For furs, I think. Look, my family owns the building, okay? I work for my family business, and they own this building."

"It's okay with me if your family's rich, Larry."

"It is? Some people find it offensive."

"Someone's bound to be rich. It's not

your fault."

They were lying in bed looking at the sunset on a Saturday evening. She kissed his head. His head had become something precious to her in the last few weeks. She loved the smell of his hair, the uneven white line of his part, the weight of his head, the view of his ears when he tucked his head beneath her chin and breathed open-mouthed on her as he fell asleep.

"Thank you for understanding," he said.

"Thank you for confiding in me."

On one very late night walking around, talking, they ended up almost in front of Laurel's building, in front of the garret, which she and Daphne had begun calling the garrotte. It was as good a time as any, with Daphne asleep in her own room, and Laurel led him up the interminable stairway.

"The garret!" he whispered. "At last." He looked up at the skylight. He had been hoping for stars, but it was opaque with a century of grime. There were stars out there somewhere, though, he knew it.

When he woke up the next morning, Laurel was already out of bed. He pulled his clothes on and went into the kitchen, which was also the living room.

"Hello," he said, and went to hug her.

"Ach! No! Larry, it's me."

"Oh. You." He gave Daphne a hug anyway. A different sort of a hug.

"She went out to buy food," Daphne said. She handed him a cup of coffee. "There's no milk. Do you take milk in your coffee? I use cream, but there's no cream, either."

Larry said he liked black coffee and settled on the futon. He watched Daphne, trying to determine how she differed from her sister, because there was a difference. If they didn't take you by surprise, by standing at the coffeepot with their back to you when you had not put your contact lenses in, there were differences. Daphne moved in shorter bursts. And as she stood staring back at him, she did not tap her foot the way Laurel always did.

"What?" she said.

"What? Nothing."

"Oh. Okay."

"Good coffee."

"My speciality. My only culinary accomplishment, as a matter of fact."

Laurel came back with a great rattling of locks and an almost empty grocery bag. "Stay there," she said. "I'll make breakfast." She threw *The New York Times* at him, and his contentment was so thorough, it made him uneasy.

"Goodbye," Daphne said, jiggling all the

134

locks open. "Tootle-oo!"

"It's so early," Larry said. "Don't you want breakfast?"

But Daphne had already closed the door and the locks were clicking back in place.

"There," said Laurel a few minutes later. She put the plate of bright, fluffy scrambled eggs on the little table.

"Oh." He stared at the eggs and looked sad.

"No good?"

"Well, it's just my cholesterol."

Laurel got out a box of cereal.

"I'm sorry," he said, sitting at the little table, his elbow on top of the half refrigerator. "Thank you for cooking them. I should have told you."

"Secrets, secrets, secrets. Your family has money, you don't eat eggs . . . What else are you hiding from me?" She gave him a bowl of cereal and a spoon, then sat beside him, the plate of eggs and toast in front of her. She ate the toast, then absentmindedly took a forkful of egg.

"Hey!" she said. "Eggs are delicious!"

"You sound surprised."

"I don't eat eggs."

"No, me, either, but —"

"I always thought there was something . . . carnal . . . about eggs." She laughed. "Exactly the wrong word. I mean, I always thought they were so gooey and . . . primal! That's the word I mean. But I wanted to make you a nice breakfast. And now I see the light! Eggs are delicious!"

"Except for the cholesterol."

"I didn't realize you have high cholesterol, or I —"

"Well, I don't. Yet."

"Because you don't eat eggs? I don't even believe all that cholesterol shit. They keep changing their minds."

"You overcame your egg disgust for me," he said. He took her hand, a little buttery from the toast, and kissed it. He smacked his lips. "Butter," he said softly. "God, one forgets."

Once Laurel began eating eggs, she began cooking eggs in earnest. She scrambled them, boiled them, deviled them, and whipped them into soufflés. She made omelets and Scotch eggs and baked eggs. She soft-boiled eggs to perfection.

"Converts," Daphne said. "They're so extreme."

Then Laurel bought an omelet pan.

"How did you know such a thing exists?" Daphne asked one dark, rainy evening when she got home. "Where did you find it?"

Laurel found it at Bloomingdale's, where everyone found everything, she said.

"And you're humming. I come home from a hard day of possessive gerund insertion, and you're cooking eggs in an omelet pan and humming?" Daphne threw her bag and then herself on the sofa. "Larry's coming for dinner, I presume."

"He doesn't eat eggs, you know that. Mr. Gravit is coming for dinner."

"Mr. Askew the headmaster? Here? Why?"

"He's been very sad," Laurel said. "He'll be here any minute."

"With the Assistant? Oh my god." She got up and rummaged through a drawer in her bedroom until she found half, almost half, of a joint. "What is wrong with you, Laurel?" she said, offering her sister a hit. "Give a girl a little warning. Jesus. Askew and Assistant Askew here. What if he figures out we switched places? And he might shed on the furniture."

But Laurel continued stirring and whisking and slicing airy, earthy mushrooms as if there were nothing out of the ordinary about her inviting her peculiar boss for dinner. "The Assistant is with her mother. Who went home to her mother. Mr. Gravit is lonely and sad and hungry. I felt sorry for him. And I wanted to try my new pan."

Daphne sidled up to her sister and gently took the knife away, took Laurel's hand in her free hand, led her to the futon, and sat her down. "Now look," she said, waving the knife for emphasis. "Look, you don't invite a man to dinner on the day his wife leaves him unless you want to fuck him, Laurel. Is that what you want to do with Mr. Gravit?"

"Don't be disgusting."

"Does he know you have a boyfriend? Does he know I'm here? That you live with a roommate? A roommate who is your twin sister?"

"Well, no, it didn't come up."

"Yeah, well, I'll bet something else came up."

"You are so disgusting. And his wife didn't leave him. She just went to see her mother."

Daphne stuck the knife into the wooden crate they used as a coffee table, then watched it wobble. "Grow up, Laurel," she said.

"I only have six eggs. Do you think that's enough?"

"I have only six eggs."

"Daphne, no one says, 'I have only six eggs.' People say, 'I only have six eggs.' "

"You don't only have eggs. You have milk. You have mushrooms. You have herbs."

"You have become such a pedant. Are six

enough? They're extra-large, but still."

"You're a disgrace."

"I know what an adverb is and where it goes, for god's sake. I, for example, am picking up a knife. I have only one sister at whom I am pointing it."

Gravit appeared at the door red-faced as well as disheveled. He was wearing his school clothes: a brown corduroy jacket and cuffed permanent-press khaki trousers, one of the cuffs partially turned down. His shirt was missing only one button, Laurel noted approvingly.

"Don't I know you?" he said to Daphne when they were introduced. "I'm sure we've met before."

Daphne couldn't tell if he was in earnest. She said, "Possibly."

"So you're something of grammarian," he said when she told him she worked as a copy editor.

"It's an uphill battle. I'm sure it is for you, too."

"Sometimes it is," he said. "But, you know, and forgive me for paraphrasing Dr. Johnson, but to paraphrase Dr. Johnson, 'To enchain syllables is just the same as trying to lash the wind — pride unwilling to measure its desire by its strength.' Pride unwilling to measure its desire by its strength. Beautiful, isn't it?"

Daphne didn't like someone paraphrasing Dr. Johnson at her. She didn't like the idea of herself as someone who enchained syllables, either.

"I just correct copy. The way you correct a student's essay. There's nothing enchaining about it."

They were sitting facing each other over the crate, he on the sagging futon, Daphne on the wooden chair they'd found on the street.

"Oh damn. That was obnoxious, wasn't it?" he said with resignation. "I'm sorry. I'm often obnoxious. That's where my daughter gets it from."

"Huh!" Daphne said, laughing.

"You've met her, then?"

Daphne shook her head. "Oh no. No, never."

"She's the light of my life, as I like to say. She's off with her mother. My wife's father is sick and they went to New Hampshire to see him. One last time, I suppose. I would have gone, but he despises me. It was awfully nice of your sister to invite me here. I did not come empty-handed!" he said, smiling suddenly, reaching into his briefcase.

Wine, Daphne thought happily. They rarely had enough money to splurge on a bottle of decent wine.

He rummaged in the briefcase. "Here it is," he said at last.

There was a magician-like gesture, and he held up something squirming and white by the scruff of its neck.

"A rabbit?"

"It's a kitty," he said in a surprisingly childish voice. "I found it on the street on my way here." He kissed its head. "A kitty cat."

A kitty cat that rose, miraculously, from a briefcase: a scrawny, mewling kitten deity. Gravit held the small god out to her in the chalice of his two cupped hands, smiled when she took it from him, uttered a soft, reverent "Kitty cat," and stood up.

"Now," he said heartily. "What's for dinner?"

To Disbra´nch. *v.a.* [*dis* and *branch.*] To separate or break off, as a branch from a tree.

— *A Dictionary of the English Language*
by Samuel Johnson

Larry's parents lived in a large, rambling house in Greenwich built in the late nineteenth century. Laurel stood uneasily among the brocade and polished wood chairs, the scattering of ornate ticking clocks, the dark portraits of unsmiling children and small dogs. Larry's family, Larry had warned her, was the kind one might have referred to as "Larry's people" if one lived in a novel written in the previous century. Larry called them Angular Anglicans, though they were Episcopalians. But it sounded better, he said, and anyway they all did have white angular faces, all those except the ones with red blotchy faces and red swollen noses,

142

which came, he said mildly, from drinking too much.

"You're just trying to scare me," Laurel said when Larry first described his "people." "With terrible stereotypes."

And here she was at a party given by the Angular Anglicans, given for her, and she was unable to shake the stereotypes from her thoughts. She watched her own parents, blandly unconcerned as they talked to a man with a red nose and a woman with a bleached Connecticut beak. How she envied them. Not the Anglicans, who were stuck talking to Arthur and Sally, but Arthur and Sally. Laurel wondered if she would ever feel comfortable at a gathering of other human beings to whom she was not closely related. Then she remembered that these strange people of distilled courtesy and ease were soon to be her relatives. She saw Daphne across the room. She wondered if they could hide somewhere together. The linen closet. The greenhouse. Surely there was a greenhouse somewhere on the property. But no, no hiding. She squared her shoulders. She prepared to mingle.

Daphne saw her sister square her shoulders, *She actually squared her shoulders!*, just as one of Larry's ancient New England–y aunts bustled past and knocked

Daphne's arm. The drink in Daphne's hand gave a shudder and spilled, cold on her skin. Drops darkened the rug. It was gin, clear as water, but it was not water. Should she get a towel and blot the spots from the rug? It was a beautiful rug, a silvery blue, very old, with the kind of worn spots that identified it as the cherished, threadbare possession of the rich rather than the cherished, threadbare possession of the poor.

She swore under her breath and headed for the kitchen, downing what remained of her drink too quickly.

The kitchen was full of attractive caterers and waiters and waitresses. Energetic young people who carried trays instead of standing on a stage. Perhaps, like Daphne, they preferred carrying a tray to acting on a stage. Perhaps they only went onstage when they could not get jobs waiting tables.

"Excuse me, sorry, oh, sorry," she said to the brave young people, realizing that however much of the gin she had spilled, a great deal too much had not been spilled and had been imbibed. By her. "Oops. Sorry. Just need some paper towels. I spilled my drink on the beautiful rug . . ."

A particularly emaciated brave young woman said, "Oh! I'll take care of that," and ran off with a dish towel without asking where the spill was.

"Darling!" a woman said when Daphne escaped to the lawn. "Where have you been hiding? What a bash this is."

"No, I'm the sister. Laurel's inside."

The woman was stylishly dressed in ill-fitting clothes, as if she had lost a lot of weight recently or gotten the dress at a deep discount.

"The sister! Of course." She stepped back and ran her eyes down to Daphne's shoes, then back to her carefully blown-out red hair. "Remarkable."

"Yes, it is," Daphne said. She wanted a cigarette. "Do you have a cigarette?"

"Oh, I quit years ago."

"Oh, *never* say never!"

The woman gave Daphne a pitying look, which Daphne tried to return.

"Well, off I go," the woman said. Her heels left a line of little holes behind her in the grass.

There were eighteen of them at the long table. Laurel sat at one end, which Daphne chose to think of as the head. Larry sat at the foot. Daphne was at his left, which she knew was an honor.

" 'How *kind* of you to let me come,' " she said.

"Why are you talking like that? In an

English accent?"

"You're supposed to say, 'Now, once again, where does it rain?' And then I sing, 'In Spain! In Spain!' "

Larry gave his goat laugh. "You girls," he said. "Is that one of your special things you do?"

"You'll have to learn our special things, Larry. Now that you're going to be one of the family."

But Daphne knew it was she who would have to learn to do without them.

"It's from *My Fair Lady*," she said. "Our favorite. Can I still say 'our'? You don't mind, do you? Of course, you two will have your own favorite musical that will be your 'our favorite,' but our 'our favorite' will still stand."

"I love *Brigadoon*."

Larry was charming and handsome, Daphne thought, but there were definite gaps.

A small dog jumped onto Larry's lap and looked around the table quizzically, clearly questioning why it hadn't been invited.

"Get her down this instant," Larry's mother said.

Daphne, just for a fleeting moment, thought Larry's mother meant her, Daphne.

Larry paid no attention to his mother. He

kissed the dog and petted her and murmured words of love.

"This instant, Larry," his mother said.

Larry pushed his lower lip out in a small pout and lowered the dog to the floor, where it lay down beside his feet with a loud sigh. Daphne felt a wave of affection for the dog, for Larry, and for her sister for seeing that, *Brigadoon* nothwithstanding, Larry was okay.

"We have a cat," she said. "I thought it was wine. Then I thought it was a white rabbit."

"I've met your cat, Daphne."

"Right. You're the allergic one."

A dispute broke out between two of the Wolfe family great-aunts. Aunt Lila was outraged at something she'd read in *The New York Times Magazine,* something about feminists — that young women didn't consider themselves feminists anymore, that it was out of fashion. Aunt Beverly, secretly called Aunt Beverly Hills by Laurel and Daphne, said, "When was it ever *in* fashion?"

"The way those people dress," one of Larry's relatives said. His uncle? Whoever he was, he had a spot on his tie. Larry's mother dipped her napkin into her water glass and rubbed at it.

"Honestly, Stuart, you of all people should not talk about the way people dress."

"Anyway, what people?" Aunt Lila demanded.

"Lesbian women," Uncle Don said. He said it casually but distinctly, the self-conscious way some people said "Jew" or "black."

"I hope they're women, Uncle Don," Laurel said. "There aren't any lesbian men, to my knowledge."

"Stop it," the man with the stained tie said to Larry's mother, who was still scrubbing. "I'm not a child."

"You interrupted me," someone said.

"Well, stop talking and I won't have to."

There were flowers in the salad. "Nasturtiums," Larry's mother said.

"What next?" Uncle Beverly Hills said. His real name was Burton. He was twenty years older than Aunt Beverly Hills. When lunch was finished, he pulled out a cigar and lit it.

Throughout the meal, throughout the day, Laurel seemed calm, happy. But Daphne caught her eye now and then and knew she was not calm at all. Was she happy? That was difficult for Daphne to know. She was too overwhelmed by her own unhappiness. She and Laurel had always shared happiness. If Laurel now took happiness for herself, as she seemed to be doing, Daphne would have to come up with a new plan.

The wedding was going to be held in Maine, near Mount Desert Island. Larry's family had a house there. They'd had it for a hundred years, or close enough, a summerhouse high on a cliff above the ocean. A house with many wings, Laurel said, and Daphne imagined it flying, all its many wings flapping. The wedding would be held at a small church nearby. Laurel didn't mind getting married in a church — such a pretty one, she said. No bleeding statues of Christ hanging from the rafters or anything. Very low-key, in perfect taste. Their parents didn't seem to mind the idea of the church, either. They were not observant Jews, after all, they said. Even the aunts didn't let it bother them. Money, old WASP money, was just like the church: in perfect taste. Daphne was the only one in the family who worried. She liked churches and loved hymns. But they were spectacles, glimpses through arched doorways, places to visit, to hear a string quartet concert or see a fresco. They weren't places in which to live out a part of your real life.

"I was sure you girls would have a double wedding," Aunt Lila said.

149

"Oh, we will," Daphne said.

The table went silent. Laurel cocked her head. "Daphne," she said. "Is there something we don't know?"

Daphne tried to smile enigmatically.

"You're such a tease," their mother said. And conversation resumed.

"But we will," Daphne said softly.

Larry would be difficult to match. He was so damn good-looking and so damn rich. Too bad he didn't have a brother. "Too bad you don't have a brother, Larry."

"Lucky you have a sister."

Daphne pondered the possibilities in the marriage department, and she was not encouraged. She was twenty-six years old — she had some time — but who among her motley collection of friends and acquaintances could possibly be the lucky man? The guys at work were unacceptable in every way. She had already slept with several of them, and they would not do, out of the question, the kind of guys who had no sheets on their beds, who washed only the tops of their plates. Or they snorted far too much cocaine. Or they scurried like rodents, unsociable, paranoid. Or they were gay. Or married already. Jon was older and had, as a consequence, more furniture and a cleaning lady who came in every other week. But he had other disqualifying characteristics. He had long been engaged to a minor Italian aristocrat, for one thing. He was a Maoist, for another. A sexy accent can carry you only so far.

It turned out that Aunt Beverly Hills was also concerned with Daphne's marital prospects. "I have a fella I want you to meet," she told Daphne a few weeks later. "I met him in Florida. He was visiting his mother. Such a nice boy. He's in manufacturing."

"I don't really want to meet a fella, in that sense."

"In what sense?"

"In the fella sense."

Daphne and her aunt were having lunch at a coffee shop. Daphne ordered a cheeseburger instead of a hamburger, knowing that her aunt would pick up the tab and so, too, the extra cost of the slice of American cheese.

"Yes, you do. That's why I asked you to lunch, dear, to tell you about this boy. He knows all about you, and he wants to meet you, so I think you should get off your high horse and go on a date with a nice fella instead of the beatniks you hang around with in Greenwich Village."

Daphne wondered if there had been a beatnik in Greenwich Village in the last twenty years and if so how she could find him and hang around with him, but she saw also that her aunt was trying to be kind, and she did not like to think of herself as someone on a high horse.

"Thank you, Aunt Beverly," she said. "Okay, I will be happy to meet your friend."

"He was visiting his mother," Aunt Beverly H. said. "Now, doesn't that tell you something?"

Within a month, Daphne was engaged. The boy who had visited his mother in Florida was named Steven Greene, and he was thirty, had his own business and all his hair. He wanted three children, but would settle for two. He did not want Daphne to work unless she wanted to. He was an excellent cook. His father was dead and his mother lived in Florida. He wasn't as rich as Larry, but he had started his company himself and someday he might be rich, you could never tell with business. Besides, money wasn't everything, as Laurel made sure to tell her when Daphne announced she was engaged.

Laurel hugged her and hugged her and they did their happy dance, the Beatlemaniac dance, they called it.

"So we will have a double wedding!" Laurel said.

"I told you."

Laurel hugged her again and said, "I think we should be neighbors. I think we have to live really close, Daphne."

"We'll have a tunnel."

"God, I've known Larry for two years. You've known Steven for a month?"

"I've decided to be the impulsive twin."

Laurel held her hands and did the Beatlemaniac dance again, then threw her arms around her. "As long as you're happy. I want you to be as happy with Steven as I am with Larry."

Daphne rested her face on Laurel's shoulder. Laurel's hair smelled different today. She sniffed.

Laurel said, "Jojoba."

"But —"

"Well, it's all-natural. And I just wanted to try something new. You don't like it?"

Daphne said, "I'm not used to it, that's all."

Daphne admired Steven. She liked him, too. He was madly in love with her, he said, though Daphne wondered if at least half that love was inspired by the fact that she was a twin. He found her twin status fascinating. He gazed with wonder at Daphne

153

and Laurel when they were together. He gazed with wonder at photographs of them when they were children. Sometimes he held Daphne's hand and stared at her fingertips, touching them gently, almost fearfully, with his own.

"Why?" she asked him once.

"That's the only part of you that's just you," he said. "Your fingerprints."

The double wedding was at the frenetic height of planning when Steven said, "That's the only part of you that's you." The identical dresses were chosen but not yet fitted. The menu was planned, but not the flowers. The date was set.

Daphne looked at her fingertips.

Laurel was a quarter of an inch taller. Should she break the bad news to Steven, that she also had the absence of a quarter of an inch that was hers and hers alone, that was her?

"I don't like the smell of jojoba," she said instead. "But I like the sound of it."

Steven kissed her fingertips.

"Let's name our first child Jojoba," she said.

The choice of tablecloths, the poached salmon, the musicians, even the service — all of it would be tasteful in the extreme.

"Mommy and Daddy don't mind the money, either," Laurel said. "They're thrilled they only have to pay out once."

"It's the least we can do. After all those outfits they had to buy two of."

"Not to mention tuitions."

"And bicycles."

"And skis. Four skis."

Daphne laughed. She thought Laurel had said "foreskins."

"Is Larry circumcised?"

"Of course he is. He wasn't born in Bulgaria."

"Good. Otherwise I don't think I could go through with it."

She couldn't go through with it anyway. Not after the fingerprint remark.

"Steven, we haven't sent out invitations yet," she told him. They were on the subway. A man across from them was leaning to the side at a sharp angle, bouncing precariously with every jolt of the train. He was smiling, eyes closed.

"My mother is trying to cut the list back," Steven said, patting her hand in a way she knew he meant to be comforting. "She promised she'd have it by next week."

"No, but my point is, there's still time to reconsider, and I have reconsidered, and I think perhaps we rushed into this idea . . ."

"This *idea*?" he said.

"Of getting married."

"Yeah, I get what the idea is, Daphne."

Silence within the noisy clatter of the train. Above the tilted, unconscious, smiling man someone had spray-painted a name in big puffy graffiti cloud letters. FOU? POY? Daphne could not make it out.

"Okay, so what *is* the idea, then? No wedding?"

Steven said. She could tell he didn't think that was the idea at all. He thought she wanted the wedding smaller or bigger or separate or sooner or later.

"That's the idea," she said.

"At all? I don't understand."

"I'm really sorry, Steven."

"You're breaking up with me? For no reason? What happened? Did something happen?"

She looked down at her shoes, at his shoes, at the blissfully unconscious man's shoes. "Look, I know it's sudden, but trust me —"

"Trust you? Oh my god. *Trust* you?"

"I'm sorry, Steven. I'm so sorry. I just don't think it will work."

He stared at her.

"You tell me this on the subway? You

break off our engagement on the subway?"

"I just —"

"For no reason. For no fucking reason."

He kept saying, "For no reason."

Daphne kept saying, "I'm sorry, I'm so sorry."

The train stopped at Fourteenth Street. He stood up suddenly. "You're not like your sister at all," he said.

As the train pulled out she saw him on the platform, giving her the finger.

There was a reason to break off the engagement with Steven, even beyond fingerprints, and his name was Michael. Something *had* happened, yes — Daphne had fallen suddenly, utterly, head-over-heels in love.

When Daphne met Michael, saw him waiting outside the Bleecker Street Theatre, she noticed he was shorter than Steven, not as thin, not heavy, just compact, and his shoes were the ugliest shoes she had ever seen, loafers with some sort of folded strap across them. Vibram soles. Normally Vibram soles alone would have turned her inexorably against him.

When he saw her he gave a little double-take, rushed up to her, and took both her hands in his.

"You're not at all what I expected," he

said, and they both burst out laughing, together. Daphne stopped thinking about his shoes. She thought about her hands, and his hands, and how her hands felt in his. She thought about the sound of his laughter and the sound of hers, joined. She took out a cigarette and when he told her she really shouldn't smoke, she smiled apologetically instead of turning on her heel as she ordinarily would have done.

"You're not what I expected, either," she said, which was true, but she also meant, *I'm not what I expected,* because she had not expected to fall in love with an old friend of Laurel's, whom she had never met before, while standing outside the Bleecker Street Theatre in the cold trying not to blow smoke his way.

Laurel had asked Michael to join them at the last minute. "You'll like him," she'd said to Daphne over the phone. "I met him at the peace march. When I got separated from you?"

She had come down to Washington from New York with Daphne and several other friends on a bus of high school students when they were sixteen. Somewhere during the day, in the marching and chanting, Laurel lost track of the others. There were hundreds of thousands of people on the

Mall, but she was suddenly alone. She had no money on her, no money to speak of. And what would she have done if she had? Hailed a cab? Take me to Larchmont, please. She was hungry and thirsty and lost, and the people all around her waving signs could have been blades of grass for all the help they were. She walked and walked, back the way she thought she'd come, looking for her bus and her friends and her sister.

After about half an hour, she realized something: she was alone. It was a new and strange sensation, being alone. Alone, even in this crowd of like-minded people. No one knows me. No one cares. No one looks at me. No one looks like me.

Oh, she thought. This is what it feels like to be alone: free!

She continued walking, aimlessly, comfortably now, strolling, watching other people as they gathered up their backpacks and signs, until she saw a bus with a piece of paper taped to its side saying ZION CHURCH NEW YORK. They were happy to give her a ride back to the city. They pointed to a seat with another white kid who had lost his bus and needed a lift, and that person was Michael. He lived hours away from Larchmont in a small town at the tip of Long Island,

and Laurel didn't see him often, but they wrote to each other for years. Whenever Laurel thought of him, she remembered that unmoored feeling of freedom.

"I know it's our sister night," she said when she called Daphne.

"Hitchcock double feature, Laurel."

"Hitchcock won't notice. And he seemed at loose ends."

"Hitchcock?"

"I knew you wouldn't mind."

Daphne had minded. Some guy Laurel hadn't seen in years? "Yeah, but it's supposed to be just us," she said. Her sister stayed at Larry's almost every night now. Daphne hated the way her voice sounded, pleading, but she continued, "No fiancés, no one but us."

"Well, he's not my fiancé, is he? He's my pen pal." Laurel laughed. "He's incredibly nice. You'll see."

And she did see. She saw Michael waiting, and then he said, *You're not at all what I expected,* and she no longer minded.

Sitting next to him in the theater, she was aware of him physically, of the distance between them, the air, as if the air were something living and breathing.

Afterward, the three of them went to dinner at a Spanish restaurant called Spain.

"I wonder if there is a hamburger restaurant in Madrid called Estados Unidos," Michael said.

Daphne was keenly aware that she had fallen in love.

"I feel so free tonight," she said.

Laurel cocked her head, looked at her, then at Michael. "Huh."

When dinner was over, Laurel said, "Let's go, sis." She took out her wallet.

"Oh no, it's on me," Michael said.

"No, no," Laurel said, pulling out some bills.

"I think I'll stay for dessert and coffee," Daphne said.

"Coffee?" Laurel said.

"Coffee."

Laurel gave her a funny look, then a funny smile, then cocked her head again, then kissed her on the cheek and said, "Huh."

While Daphne drank her strong coffee and shared a flan with Michael, a man played the guitar and a woman snapped castanets and clacked her heels on the floor.

"Too corny?" Michael said when the guitarist and dancer took a break.

"Sometimes the corniest things are the most powerful. I mean, when you don't expect them."

"Ha!" he said. He smiled, a big satisfied grin.

" 'Corny' is a funny word, isn't it?" she said. "I think it might be the least romantic word in the world."

He leaned over and whispered in her ear, "Corny."

Daphne shivered. The guitarist began to play, the dancer began to dance, her skirts swirling one way, then the other. The chords pounded faster and faster. The dancer's heels thundered.

"Corny," she whispered back, her lips touching his ear.

Their father had misgivings, but that was to be expected. Both his daughters swept away at once — it was difficult to take in. And he wished, somehow, for some reason he couldn't properly articulate, that his twin daughters were marrying other twins. Two boys who understood that Laurel and Daphne were one, two boys who were one, too. Two halves. Two sides.

Sally said, "They will take care of each other."

"I know that, but who will take care of their husbands?"

"I meant each half of each couple will take care of the other half. And vice versa."

They looked so happy these days, Laurel and Daphne. Happier than Sally had ever seen them. Her birds, untouchable, out of reach, beautiful, now seemed less like real birds than soft blue Walt Disney birds, puffs of wing tips touching as they flew off together.

"Disney is not a good omen," Arthur said.

"Bluebirds of happiness. Of course that's a good omen. And it's not meant to be an omen. It's just how I picture them."

"It's very sweet," he said. But he thought, You are imagining your daughters as cartoons.

"Omens," she said contemptuously. But there were crows gathered outside the church on the day of the wedding, and she wondered if that augured something dark and ominous.

"Crows can speak," she said to reassure herself. "They can learn words."

Don sat beside her in the church. He said, "I always knew they would turn out well."

"You always said they were freaks, Don."

"Never."

Brian, grown into a sloping, bony high school student with narrow shoulders and an earring, said, "You did."

"Brian, shut up, dear," his mother said.

"Well, Dad was right. They are freaks.

163

Freaks of nature."

"Speaking of which . . ." Sally said. She pointed her chin at the flower girl prancing down the aisle, a one-girl parade, a tiny singular Mardi Gras of white taffeta, billowing tents of petticoats, twirled licorice-black ringlets — a mythical creature, a baby Scarlett O'Hara. Rose petals preceded her, clumps of them hurled from her little fists. She was frowning in concentration. Her cheeks glowed a furious pink.

"She was one of Laurel's students," Sally whispered. "The headmaster's daughter."

"Nepotism in preschool? Academia is a dirty business," Brian said.

"Shut up, dear," his mother said again, smiling at him.

"It was kindergarten," Sally said. "Not preschool."

Now the grooms appeared. Good-looking young men, one tall and blond in a double-breasted pin-striped suit; the shorter, darker one in a three-piece dark blue suit.

"*They* didn't dress identically," Brian said. He clucked his disapproval.

Their eyeglasses were similar, though. Wire-rimmed. Gloria Steinem aviators, Sally thought. She was such a glamorous radical, Gloria Steinem. The most glamorous radical Sally could think of. The only glamorous radical she could think of, really. Emma Goldman? Hardly. Abbie Hoffman, Jerry Rubin, Tom Hayden? Well, Jane Fonda, yes. Larry and Michael did not look glamorous in their glasses, though, even if they were like Gloria Steinem's. Neither was particularly radical, either, so it all worked out, Sally decided.

She liked both boys tremendously. Larry was effortlessly polite and helpful, seeming to appear out of nowhere when a lady needed a chair pulled out, though what lady really needs a chair pulled out she could never understand, one is perfectly capable of pulling out one's own chair, a chair is not very heavy. Sally wondered if that was what had captured Laurel's heart — a tall, well-mannered boy unnecessarily pulling out her chair. That or the aviator glasses. She let out a small laugh.

"Nervous?" Don said. "It's perfectly natural."

"It's not *me* who's getting married."

Don had gotten better with the girls as they'd grown up. He spoke directly to them now with no intermediary. But they could still make him uncomfortable, and often did for the sheer joy of it. Poor Don.

The flower girl was now pirouetting toward the polished wooden lectern where the minister and rabbi stood.

"Thank you," Sally said, patting Don's hand. "I'm excited, that's all."

Don nodded sagely. He'd stopped smoking a pipe years ago, but when he nodded sagely like that, Sally could still see the pipe protruding in all its wisdom, tilted thoughtfully toward his nose. She could almost smell the sweet tobacco.

"Dear Don," she said, kissing his cheek.

And of course she *was* nervous, thank you, Don, for pointing that out. "There's nothing for me to be nervous about," she said.

She twisted away from him, toward the back of the church, looking for Arthur, for the girls, again watching the approach of the grooms. Michael smiled at her. She liked Michael. She thought she would grow to love him. The way he looked at Daphne — doting, full of humor. It was the only way to look at Daphne. It was the only way for anyone to look at someone you love. She wished she could have looked at both girls with more doting humor as they grew up. They had made her uneasy with their secret words and language games. What kind of child befriends a dictionary and tries to take it to bed with her so it will have someone to talk to? A dictionary that weighs the same as she does? Well, now they wouldn't need dictionaries in bed.

She wondered if they would teach their husbands to speak their secret language. Perhaps they had forgotten it, or pretended they had, the way her mother had pretended to have forgotten Yiddish. She hadn't heard either daughter speak a word of it for years, but she no longer knew what they got up to. The only word of Blingo, as the family had come to call their patois, they had ever taught her was "lohfo." It meant *absolutely no,* a word they thought she ought to familiarize herself with as soon as possible in her career as their mother.

The little white church in its little white simplicity looked like an art gallery that had never found its art. High ceilings. White walls. Michael felt suddenly lost, disoriented in the simplicity. He almost took Larry's hand in his. They walked beside each other, comrades marching into matrimony. Larry was all right. Daphne insisted he was not too smart. But Michael suspected Larry was as smart as anyone, just not paying attention. Like a Galapagos tortoise, he had no need to pay attention. He had no predators. He was protected by an expansive carapace of good nature, money, and family status.

The tapping of their four new shoes on

the flagstone floor was rhythmic and distinct. They were two men in a horse costume — both the tail end, Michael thought.

Larry pushed his glasses back up the bridge of his nose. His nose was sweating. He could feel the sweat running down his back, too. He smiled at his parents. His mother pursed her lips in what might have been a smile in return; his father sighed, but he was misty-eyed, Larry could see. They were not happy about the rabbi. They were not happy about the double wedding. They thought both detracted from the dignity of the occasion. Larry felt a terrible, uncontrollable laughter rising and forced it into a cough.

"All for one and one for all," Michael whispered to him.

"Three sheets to the wind!"

Michael was his new best friend. They had known immediately that that was how it had to be. As Larry did not have a best friend anymore, had not had one really since junior high school, and as Michael was a terrific sailor, Larry had been happy to comply with his fate. Michael was a little twitchy, as if he were never quite comfortable in his clothes, but Larry had always been comfortable with uncomfortable people. There seemed to be so many of them. Laurel was one. She was comfortable with him, though.

"I can be myself with you," she said to him, over and over. "I have a self with you."

Sally thought, If either girl says "lohfo" up there I'll wring her neck. It was sad that both of Michael's parents were dead, not here for this day, though it meant there would be no competition over holidays. Or grandchildren.

Larry wondered why Laurel's mother was grinning. Was she glad to get rid of her daughters? She did not fit his notion of a Jewish mother. Reserved, dry comments when you didn't expect them. His mother, WASP debutante that she was, seemed to fit the bill better — overbearing and almost possessed by her insistent, emotional energy. She frightened and embarrassed him. Sally had never embarrassed anyone, he was sure.

Brian breathed in the scent of pine trees. He'd never been in a church before, he realized with a jolt — the jolt of an outsider who has forgotten he's on the outside. As if he'd bumped his head walking into a glass door. Well, well, aren't we parochial, Brian, he thought. And we've made a pun of sorts. He had not been brought up an observant Jew, but neither had he been brought up to be tolerant of other religions. The pine scent wafting through the open windows reminded him of summer camp. He could hear bees, too, and birds. It was ridiculous, this peaceful, pretty little church. Hadn't anyone told it that Latin America could not repay its loans?

His mother blew her nose.

"What?" she said. She elbowed his side.

"I didn't say a word."

"You scoffed. Internally. I heard you."

"Quiet, you two," Don said.

Brian's father was jealous of them, the mother and son, so close. Brian knew this because his father had told him.

"But that's infantile to be jealous," Brian had said.

"Yes," his father had replied, nodding gravely.

How do you argue with someone who turns your insults into psychological insights? The only ones he ever knew to be successful were the twins. The freaks of nature. He idolized them.

Larry's parents were not, of course, the only ones who had objections to the double wedding. Arthur had told the girls it was a terrible idea the minute they suggested it.

"Why do I have to lose both daughters at once?"

"That is so old-fashioned," Laurel said.

"If you want to play that game," Daphne

said, "you'll be gaining two sons at once."

Arthur didn't want two sons. But he did want his girls to be happy, and he was worried about Daphne's impulsive decision to marry Michael.

"What if she's marrying Michael just to keep up with Laurel?" he said to Sally one night.

"It's possible."

"Who gets engaged out of the blue, then ditches the poor, pitiful schmuck for another poor, pitiful schmuck, all in a couple of days?"

"Me," Sally said. "I did."

"That was different. Different times. Girls got engaged at the drop of a hat. Now they don't even bother to get married. Why don't they live together first like everybody else? Anyway, he was no good for you, Sally. That would have been a flop, that marriage."

"I got rid of him, didn't I? I knew the minute I met you. I would have kicked an army of fiancés to the gutter to get to you."

"How romantic."

"Give them a chance, Arthur."

"Far be it from me," he said, raising his hands in surrender.

And now his daughters glided down the aisle of a church, one on either side. He walked stiffly, consciously. Through sunlight

171

and sacred shadow, the three of them approached the rabbi and the minister. Why not a swami, too, while you're at it? The windows in the church were incongruously open. Birdsong and sunlight and a soft, damp breeze came through. He felt the two arms, the two darling arms of his two daughters, his darling daughters, light and gentle on his own arms.

"I love you," he said to Daphne.

"I love you," he said to Laurel.

"We love you, too," they answered in unison. Oh, how would their husbands cope with this two-headed, redheaded spouse?

The Assistant, having run out of rose petals halfway down the aisle, flung pretend petals in front of her with increased energy. She smiled and nodded at the people in the pews, so many of them, ladies in dresses, men in suits. She stopped when she got to her parents and stared at them.

"Go on, sweetie," her mother said. "You can do it."

Do it? Of course she could do it. She shook her head in dismissal of her silly mother and resumed her work, flinging, nodding, waving. The ladies' dresses were pretty, but none was as pretty as hers. Her dress fluttered and wafted and puffed like something alive. When she reached the altar, she contemplated the two men standing there, both in black muumuus, and felt sad for them, dressed like that. She listened to the swish of her dress as she twirled. She twirled around and around until she felt dizzy, then sank down to sit surrounded by the fluffy nest of her petticoats to wait for the others to catch up.

An organ was howling out the bridal march. Finally the other marchers made it to where she sat. She looked up at the men in muumuus, waiting for the next part.

One of the brides patted her head and said, "Okay, beat it now," very softly. Was it her teacher Miss Laurel or the other one? She stared up at them carefully, trying to decide.

"Off you go, dear," said one of the muumuu men.

"Go sit with your parents now," the other muumuu man said. He was wearing a little black hat. She showed them both her basket. Didn't they know she was the flower girl?

Her father dragged her away muttering apologies, as well he should, she thought, taking her away from her wedding duties, though he seemed to be apologizing to others, not to her. There was some laughter from the ladies in dresses and the men in suits. The Assistant shrugged, which made the skirt of her dress float up and then float down like a parachute. She did it again. She had the prettiest, frothiest dress at the wedding. She was glad everyone had a chance to see it.

Her father slid into the pew after her. "You're a pistol," he said softly.

"A ship in full sail," her mother said, kissing her head.

"Perfect," the brides said later when she was eating her piece of wedding cake. "The perfect flower girl."

The Assistant smiled contentedly, a girl who was a flower, a pistol, a ship on the seven seas.

To Do´ctor. *v.a.* [from the noun.] To phys-
ick; to cure; to treat with medicines. A
low word.
    — *A Dictionary of the English Language*
                              by Samuel Johnson

Up the four flights of pea-green steps,
unlock the four locks on the pea-green door,
relock the four locks from the inside, turn
on shower, wait for hot water. I am a human being, Michael said, to himself or
aloud, who knew, who cared. I am Michael,
Michael Blumenthal, I am a human being, I
am Michael . . .
Daphne banged open the bathroom door
and squeezed in. She kicked his hospital
scrubs to a corner with distaste, then put
her arms around him.
He pressed his face into her hair. You
smell good. You are good. Did he say that

175

or think that? Thirty-six hours on call. I am Michael. You're up early.

"Yes, you are Michael." She pulled the shower curtain back and gently helped him step into the tub. "Yes, I'm up early — because I'm still up," she said. "Like you."

When he got out of the shower she dried him with a large, thin towel. It had a faded picture of a blue and orange baseball on it. It said METS.

"Meet the Mets," she sang softly. "Beat the Mets . . ."

She fell asleep as soon as they got into bed, but Michael was too tired to fall asleep. He listened to his Walkman. Laurie Anderson sang "O Superman," a chant of profundity and nonsense that washed over him like the shower, such a nice, hot shower, such a nice girl who dried him with his favorite towel, soon it would be opening day.

"Hi, I'm not home right now," Laurie Anderson said, "but if you want to leave a message, just start talking at the sound of the tone ha ha ha ha ha ha . . ." Michael had put this part of "O Superman" on their answering machine.

One night, when they got home from dinner, Daphne played back their messages and they heard, in her mother's nervous voice, the next line of the song: "Hello? This is your mother. Are you there?"

When Michael woke up, Daphne was at the kitchen table typing. Bent over like a nineteenth-century clerk. There was no self-consciousness, there couldn't be, there was too much concentration, two fingers, tapping fast, noisy as woodpeckers. Michael watched her, so absorbed, unaware of him or anything else, small tatters of paper covering the table. He tried to picture her at work at the newspaper, a moment between one pile of material to copyedit and another, gathering those moments like small change, furtively scribbling on stray bits of paper, stuffing them into her pockets to take home and type up.

Daphne was mugged once after a late close, two teenage boys, one with a knife. She had a twenty-dollar bill, the twenty-dollar bill she always kept on her for muggers, and she pulled it out of her wallet for them. They were disgusted with the wallet itself, no credit cards, and her bag was full of books and old Kleenex. Empty your pockets, they said, and from her coat flew white and fluttery shredded moths of paper, dozens of them, and the muggers laughed in surprise and left with the twenty.

Now she sat hunched over the typewriter

banging the keys with fast, violent fingers. The rackety noise was the sound of personal industry.

"Be kind," he said.

She stopped typing. "Good morning, my poor sweet sleepy one."

"Be kind to the innocent little words. They know not what they do."

"They must be taught. They must be disciplined."

"They are so small. Why can't they just go outside and play?"

"You're going to be one of those lenient, easygoing fathers, aren't you?"

"I hope so."

"Don't rush me," Daphne said, suddenly angry. "Don't rush me about kids."

Michael pulled the cat onto his lap. He frowned but did not take the bait.

"You're not even finished with your residency," she was saying. "Can you imagine what it would be like?"

Bunny the cat purred and plucked at his T-shirt. Would it be like you, Bunny? he wondered. Fluffy and self-sufficient?

"Coffee?" Daphne said, as if she were offering him a cup.

But she was not offering, he knew. He got up to grind the beans. The cat rubbed against his calves. The kettle whistled. The mystical coffee aroma filled the apartment. He poured out two cups and added cream to hers.

"Oh, all right," she said. "I'm sorry."

He handed her the cup, sat at the little table across from her and the typewriter. "You are forgiven."

"So, I guess you're not my sister," she said after a while.

"No." What was this about, what was today's tangled message? The twins were a complicated organism.

"I was really arguing with my sister," she said.

"*Laurel* is rushing you about kids?"

"No, but she will. I know she and Larry are trying. Not that she's said anything directly, but they are, I can tell."

"You count her birth-control pills?"

"I know what I know."

Michael grunted a skeptical assent, took her hand, and said, "Who am I to pretend to pierce the mysteries of twinship? But this I do know, Daphne: I'm not Laurel. And neither are you."

Daphne left the typewriter and put her arms around Michael. "How can you tell?" she said.

"She's better-natured."

Living in the apartment with Michael

179

instead of with Laurel had been strange at first. It was as if he were impersonating Laurel, his shoes on Laurel's side of the closet, his suits hanging where her dresses had been. Now she tried to remember what it was like without him.

"Laurel and I had a secret language when we were little."

"Like pig Latin, I know."

"Kind of. I wonder what it's like having a baby. It's part of you but not you. I think it must be like Webster."

"Your dog? That's not what I was expecting you to say."

Daphne drank her coffee. With her free hand she smeared the circle left by the mug on the table. "I loved Webster. I couldn't speak to him or understand what he was saying, not really, but I knew, or I guessed, and I felt so close to him. I would have thrown myself in front of a car to save him. Of course, I wasn't there when that car got him. My parents are so careless. How could they let him out the front? Do you think he was chasing a squirrel? I doubt it. That's what they said, but he was too old to be bothered with squirrels. Maybe a deer. They said they've seen deer. Everyone was excited when the deer first started showing up, but then the deer ate their flowers, so now they talk about deer as if they were rats. Maybe he chased a rat. I love Bunny, too. But he's a cat."

Michael stared vacantly at her.

"Rat," she said. "Cat."

"I thought you were going to say having a baby must be like having a twin."

"But a baby is a whole other person."

"I hate to keep harping on this, but so is your sister."

No, Daphne thought. My sister is me if I were different.

And then Laurel made herself a little bit more different. Daphne's twin sister became just a few centimeters less her twin. Laurel got her nose "fixed."

"Which is what they do to dogs when they cut their balls off," Daphne told her.

"I still have my balls, so shut up."

The nose looked fine, Daphne had to admit, although she admitted this to no one other than herself. The surgeon had made it a tiny bit straighter, more conventional. If he got paid by volume, he didn't make much on Laurel.

"Leave your sister alone," Sally said when Daphne confronted her about Laurel's nose job. "I don't know what you're so upset about. You can hardly tell the difference."

"She changed her face to make it look less like mine! Of course I'm upset. It's an implicit insult."

"Her nose was beautiful, your nose is beautiful, her new nose is beautiful. Pretend it's a sentence. Some molecules got rearranged instead of words."

Daphne started yelling into the phone. She made sentences better when she edited. She only changed something if there was something wrong with it. Or something inelegant. How could her mother not understand? Did Daddy understand? Or did he approve of this mutilation, too?

"What if your sister lost an eye in an accident?" Sally yelled back. "Would you be like this? Have a little compassion, Daphne."

Daphne slammed the phone down and went back to work. She worked all the time now. She was copyediting full-time and she was writing about copyediting. At least that's what Michael liked to say.

"No," she would say. "I'm writing about language. Grammar. Usage."

"Isn't that what copyediting is?"

"No. Copyediting is helping the words survive the misconceptions of their authors."

The column ran irregularly (like bowels, Becky said), but it was still a column. It had a byline (hers) and it had a name: The

People's Pedant. Daphne had devoted readers — fans, you might even say. The column was modishly vulgar in its attack on the vulgar tongue. *DownTown* allowed any word into print, and Daphne enjoyed the alternative journalist's privilege of tossing out "fuck"s like shiny coins to the poor. Observations, corrections, and objections that might otherwise have struck her readers as prim struck them instead as edgy. A sense of superiority does not belong exclusively to conservatives, Daphne knew.

When you have just returned from Green-Wood Cemetery, where you have buried a close friend, say, and you dig in your pocket for great handfuls of bills to release to your cabdriver who is sneezing into his own hand which he then holds out to you in order to collect his perhaps well-deserved but nevertheless exorbitant fare, it would be reasonable to expect that this viral cabdriver, having picked up a passenger at a cemetery and driven the passenger in his taxicab for close to an hour at breakneck speed broken not by necks, by the grace of God, but by brakes every few minutes as the vehicle pulls up, inevitably, behind the vehicle that precedes it on the road and has preceded it on the road for close to an hour in the bumper-to-bumper traffic, would infer from the location at which he picked up the passenger, as well as from the tears streaming down the passenger's face, that the passenger, who has just forked over a considerable sum of money, is not having an especially good day, nor is it likely that the remainder of his day will be good. It would be reasonable for you to expect that, and in these unreasonable times, you would be wrong. For, lo, listen to the cabbie as the passenger pulls the recalcitrant door handle and pushes the car door open: "Have a good day!"

Have a good day is a fucking odious formulation. I do not like to be told to have a good day, and if I did, I would not like you or anyone else, including the cabdriver, to be the one to tell me to do so. What if I don't want to have a good day? And who are you, whoever you are, to tell me what fucking kind of day to have?

Ronald Reagan is fucking president. Need I say more?

Yes, let me say more. Worse even than Have a good day is Have a good one, a new expression that has snuck up on us like TK.

Have a good one.

Have a good what? A good bowel movement? A good orgasm? A good breakfast? And why only one? Why not two? Or more?

Who are you to limit me to one?

Daphne read over what she'd written. Was the tone too petulant? Or just petulant? And what about that "TK"? Snuck up on us like *what*? And wasn't it "sneaked," not "snuck"? And shouldn't she be writing about AIDS? That was where she started, a cemetery in which a victim of AIDS was buried yesterday morning, the boy from the art department, sweet young Richie, twenty-four years old, thinner and thinner, then gone. Michael treated patients with AIDS all day long. Some of the doctors and nurses still wouldn't go near them. Bring out your dead. She remembered the grubby peasants calling that to the grubby townspeople in a Monty Python movie. So many dead. And dying. And the cabbie said, Have a nice day. A man doing his job, trying to be polite. Why didn't people just say, Thank you? Maybe the cabbie had a friend who was sick from AIDS. Maybe Have a nice day was a way of saying May God protect you, and him. Maybe. And maybe it was a way of saying, Don't bring out your dead, I don't want to see them, you must pretend that the days are nice and all the young men are not dying.

Michael was at the hospital, but he would

185

be home for dinner. She was alone with Bunny. Bunny and the Beaujolais. She poured herself a glass. The cat leaped onto her lap. The late sun came through the window, slanted and soft. The cat purred. The wine purred. She dozed off, then heard Michael's key in the first, then the second, then the third lock. She saw his tired face and got up, letting the cat slip to the floor. She poured him a glass of wine. She heard the chimes of an ice-cream truck through the window. She thought, Damn Laurel's nose. Damn that cabdriver. The cabdriver was right, it is a nice day, and I have it.

GE´NIAL. *adj.* [*genialis,* Latin.] 1. That which contributes to propagation.
— *A Dictionary of the English Language*
by Samuel Johnson

Hackneyed phrases, said the great grammarian Henry Watson Fowler, author of *A Dictionary of Modern English Usage,* have become hackneyed because they are useful. This sentiment was, of all things, what Laurel thought of when she found out she was pregnant. Right after she thought, Pregnant pause.

She left the doctor's office, went to a phone booth, and called Daphne. "I'm coming to see you right now."

There was a pause. A pregnant pause! Laurel thought.

"What's wrong?"

"Nothing at all. Just some news."

187

Another pregnant pause.

"You're pregnant!"

"This phone booth smells so much. I'll be right over."

"You're the first one I'm telling," she said when she got there. Pregnancy, wombs, babies — they seemed somehow to have more to do with her sister than with her husband. "I haven't even told Larry yet."

"Oh, Laurel." Daphne embraced her and whispered awed congratulations, then began to cry.

"Don't worry," Laurel said.

"I know."

Daphne tried not to show how moved she was by being the first to hear the news. She scrutinized her sister's face.

"What?" Laurel put her hand up to her nose.

"No, no, I'm looking to see if your face is glowing." She wondered how long Laurel had suspected. For at least a month. Yet she had never mentioned it.

"You glow later. Now you puke."

"Remember when we went on the grape-fruit diet?" Daphne said.

Laurel now put a hand on her stomach. "You can't see anything yet."

"No."

But soon Laurel's belly would expand and

Daphne's would not. When they'd gone on the grapefruit diet, they tried to lose weight at exactly the same rate. Neither of them had needed to lose any weight at all, and neither of them did.

"I still like grapefruit," said Daphne.

"Someone gave us grapefruit spoons for a wedding present."

"Trade you the electric knife."

But Laurel didn't want an electric knife. She never wanted to eat again, she said. Everything made her feel sick. Nothing was palatable.

Especially not an electric knife, Daphne said.

Laurel smiled at that. And when Larry was out of town for one of the Lamaze classes, Daphne came with her instead. The rest of the couples laughed in delight when they saw the twin sister with the same flaming red hair.

"Our lives will change, I guess," Laurel said when they left the Y where the classes were held. "I mean, they already have. But now they'll change more."

"There will just be an extra person in the family. And I will be an aunt. That's not so radical."

"No."

They walked along in the early dark of

February. The cold was raw, and bits of gray snow littered the gutters. Laurel stopped to pull her gloves on. She said, "Daphne, I have to tell you something."

"The baby's not mine."

"We're moving to the Upper West Side. We're buying an apartment. We found a beautiful place, we just have to tear down some walls all the therapists put up, and then it will be perfect and it's on Eighty-Ninth Street."

"You can't! That's so far away. There's no direct subway line. You're moving to a cultural wasteland. Oh, this is bad, Laurel. This is bad."

She stomped up the street, then stomped back.

"Shit."

"I know, but with the baby coming . . ."

Daphne pulled out a pack of cigarettes, held it out to her sister.

"I can't smoke. I can't drink. I can't even drink coffee. Come on, be happy about this. I mean, not that I can't drink coffee. But the apartment — it's a big, wonderful apartment. We couldn't live in Larry's fur-vault apartment forever. You'll move, too, as soon as Michael gets done with his internship."

"Residency."

"Okay. Residency. Then you can move

190

right next door."

"Djever."

"Djever day djever."

Daphne thought of the woman on the lawn at Larry's parents' house, the woman whose expensive clothes didn't fit, whose heels sank into the soft turf. That cheered her up, she could not have said why. "You're right." And there would be a baby. A nephew or a niece. It would idolize her, the fabulous, glamorous downtown aunt.

The next sisterly trial for Laurel was the moment she had to tell Daphne that she was leaving work. Laurel hemmed and hawed.

"So, um . . . Hem. Haw."

"What? What's the matter?"

They were sitting on a bench in Riverside Park near the new apartment and watching robins hopping on the patchy grass.

"I'm hemming and hawing."

"Yes, I hear that, Laurel."

"Because I don't want you to be mad at me, and, even more important, I don't want you to lecture me."

"Spit it out," Daphne said.

"Oh," she said when Laurel told her. She took a deep breath and said, "But you like teaching," though when she thought back to her one day as Miss Wolfe the kindergar-

191

ten teacher, there was a part of her that did not blame Laurel for quitting. "But I guess if teaching is too, you know, unsatisfying, um, intellectually, you can get another job."

"I don't want another job. I like teaching. But I want to be home with my own child, not chasing other mothers' kids around."

"Do you realize how selfish you sound?"

"No."

"But, Laurel, a child needs a strong, interesting, engaged mother. Not a boring housewife."

"A child needs a mother."

And you know what? Laurel did not say, but thought in a thunderous voice: A mother needs a child.

"Babies don't even talk."

"We did."

Daphne was chain-smoking. Laurel turned to avoid the smoke.

"Oh my god! You're such a stiff! It's just smoke. Talk about lecturing."

"You need to quit. You really do."

"No one ever quits. A wise colleague told me that."

"You can't smoke in the apartment when the baby comes, Daphne."

Daphne shook her head. "You are becoming so conventional. Radically conventional. Just don't turn into a Republican."

Laurel laughed. "No."

"Okay, then you can stop teaching."

"It's only kindergarten."

Daphne, of course, agreed with her. But she didn't want to hurt her feelings. "Kindergarten is the cradle of civilization," Daphne said stoutly.

They spoke on the phone every day.

"But what is a telephone, anyway?" Laurel said one day, pulling the receiver away from her ear, looking at it. She was lying on the couch in her new apartment, spring sunlight wafting through the windows. "I mean, how does a telephone work? It's practically obsolete, but I still don't know how the words squeeze through the wires."

"It's electricity."

"Why don't the light switches talk, then?"

This was the kind of conversation they had most days. The telephone, previously not that important for the inseparable twins, became vital, an extension of intimacy. Sometimes they barely said a word, attached just by the knowledge of attachment.

But as Laurel watched her belly grow rounder, she also began to notice a difference in the phone calls from her sister. While Laurel lolled in nauseated lethargy on the living room couch, Daphne was working harder than ever. Laurel noticed that as she faded from the world into a physical and mental lassitude she had not believed possible without the aid of quaaludes, Daphne burned with the vivid fires of ambition and industry.

Daphne was finding more and more success, too. Laurel knew what was coming as soon as she picked up the phone and heard her sister's voice: the exultation, the self-doubt, the need. The excitement and gratification that came with her success did not appear to satisfy her for more than a minute. Success seemed only to stimulate her craving for success.

She was a clever writer, and people seemed to love to be scolded about grammar. Daphne was becoming the Miss Manners of modern speech, examining a new word usage or a neologism like an exacting governess judging the curtsies of her charges. She was serious about her writing, more serious than was good for the column, in Laurel's opinion. It could have used a little levity, real levity, less sarcasm and sniffy superiority. But Daphne was serious about every word she wrote, as well as the fact that she wrote them. Kee-riste, Laurel thought sometimes, remembering Uncle Don and the collection of words in the childhood notebook.

"Laurel, Laurel, guess what?" Daphne on the phone, breathless with importance.

Laurel could not guess what, only that the what was something good, a bigger assignment or a letter to the editor praising something Daphne had already written, from someone famous, perhaps.

"What?" she said. "Tell me."

"*Vogue!*"

"*Vogue?* Like, the magazine?" She tried to imagine her sister, who still favored a somewhat ratty punk look, in a big color spread in *Vogue.*

"*Vogue* like the magazine! They want me to do a piece on fashionable words. Not words about fashion, but words or phrases that are fashionable right now. I have been asked to write for *Vogue!* They pay a dollar a word! They want a thousand words! I'll be a thousandaire!"

Laurel felt the quick needle of envy. So childish. And she had so rarely felt envious of Daphne as a child. Pull that ugly, germy needle from your sisterly arm, Laurel, for heaven's sake! she thought.

Without too much effort, she let her happiness at Daphne's success wash over her. Daphne deserved this success. She worked hard, coming home late from her job to sit at the typewriter and bang out warnings about the linguistic apocalypse. Oh shut up, Laurel, you're getting as sarcastic as The People's Pedant. She listened with real sympathy then to Daphne's exhausted, worried, exalted lament.

Laurel, herself, was exhausted, too — exhausted, plain and simple. Most of her days were spent lying on the couch, staring up at the living room light fixture. It was an old round dish of frosted glass attached to the ceiling by an invisible mounting, reverse gravity, or possibly chewing gum. The light fixture had probably been there since 1929, when the building was put up. Laurel could see shadows inside it, the ghostly remains of flies and moths that had come for the bulb and stayed for eternity. Or at least until she asked the building's super to bring a ladder so she could dust the small corpses out. The super was a kind man and would insist on doing it for her and would refuse any payment. But she did not call him. Every day she did not call him. The effort of calling him was too great. And if she did somehow find the energy to call him and he did bring his ladder and climb it and clean out the deceased, what would be left for her to look at? This was her life now, she couldn't give it up. Contemplation of a filthy frosted glass ceiling light and its insect decay was time-consuming and enervating, but it was hers.

"I'm enervated," she said after soothing and congratulating her sister. "I like that word because it sounds like it means the opposite of what it means."

"I'm going to think of you as languid," Daphne said. "It's more classical and dignified."

"I am the opposite of dignified. I'm wearing yellow overalls. I borrowed them from Alison. She had her baby six months ago. She has a closet full of maternity clothes in primary colors."

"What do you do all day?"

"I pretend I'm not here."

"Well, can you think of any words for my piece?"

"No, Daphne. I am a vegetable that is incubating a mammal. That's all I can do, incubate. You can come uptown and watch me gestate, if you want. You could listen to the common folk speak their new dialect on the subway. It would be research."

"Can I show it to you when I'm done?"

"Sure. You know another word I like? 'Restive.' It sounds like the opposite of what it means, too."

"If I ever get it done. What if I can't finish it?"

Laurel assured her she would finish. She always finished what she started.

"But this is different. This is national. This is a big break for me."

Laurel affirmed that national was a good thing, different was a wonderful opportunity, a big break was a big break.

"Yeah, I guess I'll finish, but what if I don't? And what if I do and it's bad?"

No, Laurel was sure it would not be bad. It would be good.

"They could reject it . . ."

Daphne went on for a while about the various ways she could fail in the composition of the article for *Vogue*. "And anyway, *Vogue* is a stupid fashion magazine. It's true they print things by serious writers, like Alfred Kazin and Elizabeth Hardwick, I mean it's pretty prestigious, but I don't know if that's the kind of prestige I really want, I mean I'm serious about what I write, but what if I can't do it and they don't like it . . ."

Laurel turned her eyes from the ceiling light to her stomach, a buttercup prominence that rose in front of her, a hillock that blocked her view of her feet.

"Okay, yes, it's such a big break," her sister was saying. "I mean, it's *Vogue*, it's really prestigious, they pay, it could lead to other things. You don't think I'll blow it, do you?"

Laurel might have drifted a bit, drifted as in fallen asleep. She noticed that her sister was still talking but now sounded testy.

"Why are you ignoring me? Why aren't you helping me?"

"Well, let's see, fashionable words . . . People have started saying 'asshole' a lot more than they used to. 'Douchebag,' too, that's quite à la mode."

"Thanks," Daphne said. "Thanks a lot."

"You're welcome." She hung up and resumed her examination of the light fixture. "Asshole" and "douchebag" really were much more commonly used than they had been when Daphne and Laurel were growing up. "Asshole," she said out loud. What an awful word. She wondered if Daphne would hyphenate it. She should have asked.

Daphne examined her list of words. "State-of-the-art"? Not very sexy. "Stressed-out"? "Skanky"? "Multitasker"? They were contemporary words, they described much of contemporary life, but *Vogue* was not about contemporary life. It wasn't about life at all. It was about a fantasy of a fantasy. Where would she find those fantasy words?

People fantasize. We will go among the

people, as our sister suggested. We will go on the subway, but we will notice that no one speaks on the subway. It is far too noisy. And they are all listening to their Walkmen. Is "Walkmen" the plural of "Walkman"? Or should it be "Walkmans"? A topic for a column. The day is not wasted! Since Daphne had begun writing, she noticed that she always felt she was falling behind. But it was not necessarily clear to her what exactly she was falling behind, which made it difficult to determine how she might catch up and pull ahead. Well, anyway, we have moved forward today, she told herself. But why are we always talking to ourselves in this manner? Has everything become fodder for our work? Are we more observant than we were when we were simply copyediting? Or are we self-consciously appropriating our own life? Are we no longer an authentic person? Do we care? Why are we thinking in the first-person plural?

She exited the subway at Eighty-Sixth Street and wandered into a few stores before her visit to Laurel. The Foot Locker was crowded with young teenage boys and their mothers. Daphne pretended to examine the different sneakers.

"These are tight," a boy of about eleven

said. He was wearing bright orange sneakers.

"Should we try a bigger size?" his mother said.

"Mom." He bestowed on her a look of scorn.

"But if they're too tight . . ."

"It means cool, Mom. They're cool, okay?"

Daphne walked happily toward Riverside Drive. She loved the word "tight." It meant so many different things that were all somehow the same thing. Tight muscles. Tight with money. Money is tight. The organization is tight and well run. Tight friends. Tight-lipped. Hold tight. Sleep tight. Of course it also meant tipsy, which made less sense. And apparently it meant cool, too. Better than "groovy," anyway, a word she shamefully remembered using freely. A kind of progress, then, in the world.

The apartment was in a big prewar building that had just gone co-op the year before. The lobby was decorated with old cracked tiles. The elevator had to be run by an elevator man who closed the gate and pulled the lever to start an ascent or descent just like an elevator man in a department store in a black-and-white movie. All of the elevator men who worked there were related, looked alike, and never gave up hope for the Mets.

201

They recognized Daphne. She was the one with the flat belly.

Laurel answered the door looking . . . Daphne struggled for a word to describe her sister. Certainly not "tight." "Slatternly," perhaps.

"No one says anything on the subway, so that was no help," Daphne said. She sat down in one of Laurel's chairs, a Bauhaus chair, Larry had once explained, a contraption of straps and cowhide that was surprisingly comfortable. Laurel resumed her beached-whale posture on the couch. She was wearing the alarming bright yellow overalls she had described before.

"Do you go out in those?"

"Yeah."

"Wow."

"I just go to Fairway to buy avocados. That's all I can eat. You know, if you're really looking for fashionable words, that's where you should go. Food is all anyone talks about. All our friends. It's nauseating. Couscous. Kiwi fruit . . ."

Daphne had jumped to her feet. "My god, Laurel!" She raised her hands toward the ceiling. "Hallelujah! Hallelujah! My sister is a genius!"

"Radicchio?"

"Laurel! You have saved my life!"

"*Fraises du bois,* fucking frisée, *beurre* fucking *blanc.* Is there nothing else to talk about?"

Daphne embraced her sunshine-yellow, beached-whale sister. "No! There is nothing else to talk about! The piece is writing itself."

"Crostatas and crumbles and croissants," Laurel said with disgust. "Well, not croissants so much anymore. Arugula, though. I thought people were saying rugelach. Fiddlehead ferns. Feh."

"You are such a good sister. You're a genius! And I have the same genes! I am so lucky. Yes, of course, it's all food. Fashion is food. Food is fashion. I have to go write my piece now! Why didn't I think of this? Because I didn't have to because you are a genius."

"Because you are not sick to your stomach every time someone extolls the virtues of raspberry vinegar."

Daphne squeezed onto the couch, kissed her sister's forehead, and offered to get her a cracker.

"Seafood sausage," Laurel said. "Now, that is a disgusting concept. They're white and pallid. And fishy. And blueberry mayonnaise . . . Oh god . . . Excuse me." She pushed Daphne aside, got up, and disappeared down the hall, presumably to vomit in one of the bathrooms. Daphne envied her the bathrooms. Two bathrooms. Two bedrooms. A maid's room. A dining room. A living room. A front hall, for god's sake. While Daphne still lived in their little tenement walk-up. As soon as Michael finished his residency, they would be able to afford something better. Though she would never want to live on the Upper West Side. Maybe Tribeca, if she could figure out exactly where it was.

Laurel returned and resumed her position on the couch. "I know I should exercise. Do you think that was exercise?"

"Plenty."

"Good. Oh!" she called as Daphne left the apartment. "Sushi! And cheese! People talk about cheese *a lot,* right? Goat cheese. Not Brie. Brie is passé."

To celebrate the imminent arrival of the first grandchild, Sally and Arthur decided to hold a family brunch.

"Just like the old days," Sally told Laurel on the phone. "Your aunt and uncle will come. Brian will come. And the best part is, you won't have to move. We will all come to you, and we'll bring everything with us."

"You don't have to import bagels and

lox," Laurel said. "This is the epicenter of the bagel and lox trade."

"Let me spoil you, honey."

Arthur got on the phone. "Let your mother spoil you."

"Spoil you with second-rate suburban smoked salmon and soft suburban bagels," Daphne said when her sister told her about the brunch. She was deep into her piece about fashionable food, none of which originated in Westchester. "Please," she added. "Pleeaase don't make me come."

"Oh no, you can't blow this off and leave me and Larry alone with all of them."

The subways, Daphne said, the dreary conversation, pompous Don and snarling Brian, Paula and their mother whispering in the kitchen . . . "Spare me," she said. "Please, oh please, spare me. This will take up my whole day. It will be so boring and so time-consuming. I have so much work."

"We *always* do this *together,*" Laurel said. She was shocked. How could there be a family get-together without Daphne? How could Daphne even consider ditching this brunch, ditching her family, ditching Laurel?

"You can't do this, Daphne. It's against the rules of nature. And it's just shitty. To me."

"They don't need me," Daphne said. "It's not *me* they're celebrating. *I'm* not pregnant."

Laurel had been silent, wounded. And furious. That lousy little workaholic sister of hers, deserting her. "You're leaving me with the weight of Larchmont on my weary, pregnant shoulders. You should be ashamed!"

"Your shoulders aren't pregnant. *You* should be ashamed!"

Then Daphne gave a little cough. It was what she had always done as a child when she made up an excuse. Cough. "I'm on deadline," she said. "Deadline, okay?"

Laurel said, "Oh, fine," and slammed down the phone. But it was not fine. And they both knew it.

Uncle Don drove the family in from Westchester. While he tried to park, Laurel's parents and Aunt Paula bustled in the kitchen, and Brian slouched toward the couch, listening to his Walkman. Laurel waved at him. He waved back.

"I brought extra cream cheese," Sally said. She carried in a platter piled with pale, puffy bagels. "It's whipped. Temp Tee! Daphne always liked Temp Tee."

"She liked the name, Mom. But thank

206

you, that was very thoughtful."

"Well, I *love* whipped cream cheese," Larry said. "Less fat."

"Anyway," Laurel said, "Daphne and Michael can't come."

Sally looked alarmed. "Why not?"

"Brian, take that headset off," Don said as he walked in. "This minute."

"She has a deadline."

"Brian!" Don was tapping his son's head with his car key, a long, thin Volvo key. The Citroën was long gone.

"A deadline? I'll give her a deadline," Arthur was saying. "We drove all the way in and she can't come uptown to see her family?"

"You come in all the time."

"Well, your aunt and uncle don't. We went to a lot of trouble. Your aunt made her coffee cake."

"Physical abuse is not necessary," Brian said, loudly, the way one does with headphones on. He slapped his father's hand away.

Don lifted them from his son's head. "Turn off the music and behave."

Poor Brian, hauled into the city on a Sunday to sit miserably among his kin. Maybe Laurel and Brian could sneak out and go have brunch with Daphne down-town.

"I don't understand her," Arthur said.

Laurel thought, She's selfish and inconsiderate. What's to understand?

Larry said, "A deadline is a deadline. I guess."

The components of the word "deadline" struck her. A line that is dead. No, a line that you must not cross or you will be shot dead. From prisons in the Civil War. Was that right? She would look it up later.

They settled at the table, and Laurel, who had veered recently into a ravenous stage in her pregnancy, slathered cream cheese and piled salmon and red onions and capers and tomatoes on a bagel, admiring all the colors. "I'm eating for two," she said.

Brian looked at her with sudden interest. "You're having twins?"

"No, Brian. Me and the baby. That makes two."

"Oh, right."

"Genius," Uncle Don said.

"Fraternal twins run in families," Brian said, glaring at his father. "But identical twins don't, that's all. So it would be interesting."

Laurel had a sudden desire for scrambled eggs. Larry offered to make her some.

"Don't take advantage of him," Sally said, handing her the platter of salmon. "Eat this."

"You know a lot about twins," Laurel said to Brian.

"I know a lot about a lot of things."

She remembered Brian putting pebbles in his mouth and chanting, "China, china, china." He had acquired a certain snarling high school dignity these days, and she tried to smile at him in a way that showed her sympathy, but he didn't glance in her direction.

"Now, this business about Daphne," Uncle Don said. "I'm surprised she didn't join us, I really am. Is there some sort of rift between you?" he asked almost hopefully.

"Oh, Don," Aunt Paula said.

"It's a transitional time," he said. "A rift would be quite natural."

"No, god, Uncle Don. Not a rift. A deadline."

"A deadline," he said, obviously unconvinced.

"Well, *I* think Daphne is being very rude," Sally said.

"You've never had deadlines," Aunt Paula said. "Believe me, they wait for no man. And especially for no woman."

"Yes, Mom has deadlines all the time," Brian said. "At court, at the office. Deadlines make her late for everything at home." He seemed quite pleased announcing his mother's delinquency. "She misses a million family things."

"I do, it's true," Paula said complacently.

"Hey, Dad," Brian said, turning with a grin to his father. "Is there a *rift*? Is there a rift between you and Mom?"

Laurel laughed. Brian, about to start college, was as annoying as ever, but now he was annoying the right people. She noticed a plastic container of pickles that had not yet been opened. She popped the top off and saw that the pickles were bright half dills. "Oh thank you, thank you. Half dill. You know how we pregnant ladies like pickles."

"All anyone in this family really cares about is food," Brian said. "In Ethiopia people are eating grass at this very moment. Have you even read the EPA report on the greenhouse effect?"

"He's nervous about going off to Cornell," Don whispered to Laurel.

"Sweetheart, eat your bagel, then put your headphones back on and listen to your music and leave the poor, ignorant grown-ups alone," Paula said.

"If there's a rift," Uncle Don was saying to Daphne, "you know you can always talk to me."

"What if there's not a rift? Can I talk to you then?"

"Oh god," Arthur said wearily. "Don't start."

"Tell your daughter that she can talk to me anytime she feels it necessary, providing she keep a civil tongue in her head."

"Laurel, leave your poor uncle alone," Sally said. "What is wrong with you two?"

As Brian sloped back to his Walkman and the living room couch, Laurel noticed a happy smirk on his face, and she felt, somehow, that even without Daphne the brunch had been a success.

ONE. *adj.* [an, œne, Saxon; *een,* Dutch; *ein,* German; ἓυ, Greek.] 1. Less than two; single; denoted by an unite.
— *A Dictionary of the English Language*
by Samuel Johnson

The word "baby" comes from *babulus,* which means *prattle* in Latin. Laurel told Charlotte that.

"I can prattle to you, and you will understand," she said in a soft, prattling voice.

The second meaning of "baby" in the dictionary was *a doll or puppet.* Laurel did not mention that to Charlotte.

She took her to Riverside Park every day. They walked through a rotunda and an underpass beneath the West Side Highway and made their way to the river. ("Well, only you walk," Daphne said when told of their outings. "The baby rolls in her carriage.")

As autumn took over, the walk got colder. Small gray waves splashed against old pylons. It was a lonely place, or it would have been lonely without Charlotte. With Charlotte, it was full.

Imagine, she said to the baby, not bothering, not needing to speak out loud: *just one of you.*

But she could not, in fact, imagine. For her, there had always been Daphne. And now Daphne's place, a place that was neither inside nor outside of Laurel, was occupied by this child.

"You understand me," Laurel said to the baby.

The wind picked up and Laurel tucked the blanket closer around the now-sleeping child, careful not to disturb her.

They really should have named the baby Privity, she thought, for there had never been anyone closer to her. There had never been anyone she loved as much. Of course, they could not really name her Privity. Even in the singular it sounded like a legal principle. Or a hedge. Or a toilet.

"Privity," Laurel said to Charlotte. She was fast asleep in the lacy white blanket that someone had crocheted, she wished she could remember who, probably one of Larry's aunts or former girlfriends or his parents' housekeeper, there were so many people now in their family circle, though no one mattered except this little baby. No part of the baby was visible except her face, which looked a little chapped, the pink of her cheeks like an old man's reddened skin. Laurel turned the carriage around and headed toward home. Her hands were cold, and she reached into the pocket of her coat for her gloves, but she had forgotten them.

They had named the baby a proper name, a beautiful name that Laurel had always wished were her own name: Charlotte. Every young couple they met seemed to have named their daughter Charlotte, too, but Charlotte didn't seem to mind.

Both sets of grandparents were forever hanging around the baby, like hyenas around a dead thing.

"That's a horrible thing to say," Larry said. "Jesus, I'm going to have nightmares."

"Jackals."

"They're grandparents, honey. They just want to see her and hold her."

"And suck up her life force."

She didn't mean her parents, though she would never tell Larry that. It was his parents.

"They hover and snarl, drooling with savage grandparent hunger. Your mother comes every single day. Nearly."

"She helps, though, doesn't she? I hope she does."

Laurel said, Yes, of course she does, they were incredibly lucky.

Larry's mother was generous and extreme, a physically slight person, slender and graceful, but a large presence. She arrived at the door burdened with noisy, crackling paper grocery bags overflowing with food. In this way, she was the kind of woman Laurel tried to avoid on the West Side, the ones tailgating other shopping carts in Fairway, elbowing past you at the counter at Zabar's. Larry's mother was a menace in the aisles of a specialty grocery store, steely-eyed and single-minded. But once inside her son's apartment with the spoils of war, she became as calm a person as, with her composed expression and confident smile, she initially seemed to be.

"She's not even Jewish," Laurel said to Larry. "How did this happen to her? This deli-gathering hunter-warrior persona? She doesn't act like this in Bar Harbor."

He laughed. "No. She's environmentally sensitive."

Laurel made tea for her mother-in-law and served whatever tidbits had been captured on that day's foray. Then they put

Charlotte on the table in her basket and watched her as if she were a television show.

"Her feet!"

"She's laughing!"

Sometimes Laurel snuck a glance at her mother-in-law. How happy she was, placing her manicured hands over her eyes, removing them with a cry of "Peek-a-boo," an ancient game that Charlotte thought was new, new again, and again, new!

I helped make someone this happy, Laurel thought. Someone who is now my family. Someone I hardly know. She meant her mother-in-law, but she realized she meant Charlotte, too.

Arthur sometimes said Laurel and her family should have moved closer to them, to Westchester.

"You come almost every day as it is, so what are we talking about here? Every hour?"

"How can they move to a soulless suburb and leave behind the single-room-occupancy hotel down the street?" Sally said to the baby. "That would never do for your mommy, would it? But we wouldn't mind, would we? Because we would have *you* in our soulless suburb."

"You see her a million times a week, Mom."

Sally examined the baby's fingernails, tapping them with her finger, which looked enormous beside Charlotte's, the finger of a giantess. "Her fingernails are little bits of shell."

Laurel said, "They get so sharp. Tiny little pearl claws is more like it. I just trimmed them."

"Your mommy likes to shock her mommy, Charlotte. That's why she said you have claws."

Laurel laughed.

Sally pressed the baby's toes to her lips and said, "What about your sister?"

"I don't cut her fingernails."

"Does she come up to see you? Which you know is what I meant."

"Of course she does," said Arthur.

"Of course she does," Laurel said.

Daphne did not come uptown often, though. Becky had been promoted to managing editor, and Daphne had taken her place as copy chief. The *Vogue* piece had been a success, and she was writing more than ever for *DownTown,* too. She had visited Laurel a couple of weeks ago, but that was what it felt like to Laurel, a visit, and Laurel had sensed herself becoming self-conscious, awkward with her sister.

As Daphne kissed and fondled Charlotte, Laurel had been unable to stop herself from weakly asking for reassurance. "You like her, don't you?"

Daphne had removed her face from Charlotte's belly. "You nut. I adore her. I want her. How is it I got the stray cat and you got the gorgeous baby?"

That had been a relief, to hear her say that.

"And she has red hair, so we know you're the mother," Daphne had continued. "Although, who's to say it wasn't me in that hospital bed swearing and sweating?" She lifted Charlotte and held her out, examining her. Then, with a satisfied smile, she said, "Yup. She has my nose."

Now Laurel smoothed the wisps of baby red hair on Charlotte's brow, stroked the baby's nose, which was indeed a tiny replica of the twin nose she had once had, and said to her parents, "Daphne doesn't come up here every fifteen minutes like you two, and I do miss her. But it's different these days."

Sally picked up the baby and held her close. "Things are different," she said in a singsong. She rested her cheek on Charlotte's head. "Things are different." Things *were* different now with this grandchild in her arms. There had been so little time to spare when her daughters were this young. So little time to rest a reverent cheek on a small, tender head.

To WORK. *v.n.* pret. *worked,* or *wrought.*
[*peoρcan,* Saxon; *werken,* Dutch.] 5. To
ferment.
— *A Dictionary of the English Language*
by Samuel Johnson

Charlotte is born in October. The assumption is, among some, that having successfully produced her offspring, Laurel will now long to return to the classroom in January. But she does not.

"You're burying yourself," Daphne says. "You know the school would love to have you back, Laurel."

"Indeed we would," says Headmaster Gravit.

It is a dinner party. An ambush party, Laurel thinks.

"You had a semester off. How much time do you need to devote to changing disposable diapers?"

Oh, Gravit, Laurel thinks as the headmaster's unbuttoned cuff skims the gravy on his plate.

"Darling." Gravit's wife, Pamela, dabbed at him with her napkin. "And if she's not ready to come back, she's not ready to come back."

Everyone is speaking at once, gesticulating, shaking their heads, all of it aimed at Laurel.

"You don't understand," she says. "You don't understand."

"You're withering on the vine."

"I think Daphne means you have so much to offer." Michael, not at all convinced that is what Daphne meant.

"No, I meant she's withering on the vine."

Laurel is becoming angry. Larry senses it and says how nice it is to have a traditional Christmas dinner when it's not even Christmas yet. Turkey, stuffing, pumpkin pie. He is about to say, And with no relatives, but remembers Daphne is the very closest and the most troublesome of all the relatives. "Shall I check on Charlotte?" he asks. No one hears.

"I'm being a mother." Laurel is speaking as loudly as a person can speak without yelling. "What's wrong with that? 'To mother'

— it's a verb, something you *do.*"

"You have nothing to talk about anymore." Her sister again, even louder. "You need to go back to work!"

"You do know you're an extraordinary teacher?" Gravit, blandly, as if this were not part of an argument, just a random compliment.

Laurel pushes back her chair with a great clatter and storms into the living room.

"Oh dear."

"Oh, Larry, don't worry, I am not having a tantrum."

She pulls a small red-bound volume from the bookshelf.

"The *Institutio Oratoria* by Quintilian," she says. "*You* gave me this book, Gravit."

"Yes, but —"

" '*Above all . . .*' " she reads, loudly, firmly. " '*Above all, see that the child's nurse speaks correctly.*' " She waves the little red volume at them. "Thus spake Quintilian."

"But our child doesn't have a nurse," says Larry.

"That's my point, Larry."

"And who are we to question Quintilian, whoever he is, when he's at home?" Daphne. She crosses her arms. Smug expression. Why does ignorance make you feel superior, Daphne? Laurel thinks.

"He wrote a treatise on education in the first century," Gravit says.

"And he said the nanny should be a philosopher. Where the hell am I going to find a philosopher nanny? And failing that, you have to find someone with good character, obviously, but, and I quote, 'they should speak correctly as well. It is the nurse that the child first hears, and her words that he will first attempt to imitate.' "

"You're afraid Charlotte will have a nanny accent?" Pamela Gravit, a little shocked.

"Quintilian continues, and I quote: 'We are by nature most tenacious of childish impressions, just as the flavour first absorbed by vessels when new persists, and the colour imparted by dyes to the primitive whiteness of wool is indelible.' "

"Laurel! You're a horrible snob," Daphne cries out.

"But I'll go off to work and teach other people's children and come home to some babel of Oliver Twist, Lucky Charms, Peter Tosh, Boris Badenov, Topo Gigio . . ."

"Pepé le Pew. You forgot Pepé le Pew, you horrible xenophobe. Yes, yes, we must perpetuate the purity of accent of our forefathers, the noble people of Larchmont, for there alone lies truth and beauty . . ."

They are all laughing, and laughing at her.

Not one of them understands, not even Larry. Not even Daphne, Daphne least of all, with her hungry careerism, her judgments and decrees. Not even me, Laurel thinks. Do I care how a baby pronounces baby words? No. But I want to be there to hear them however she says them. I want to stay home with my baby and hear her. I want to stay home with Charlotte.

"The worst defense for stay-at-home motherhood ever," Daphne is saying. "Protect the child from the bad pronunciation influences of the lower classes. Because we are such aristocrats!"

And there is more laughter, and Laurel knows what she sounds like. "I know I sound crazy or even worse . . ."

"Worse," they all say.

"But language matters, doesn't it?" She turns desperately to her husband, to her headmaster, to her sister. "Doesn't it?"

It does, it is what holds us together and tears us apart. Why is her own language failing her now? Why can't she just say what she means? That she wants to be there for every word, every sputter of meaning and need, every demand, every refusal, every discovery of every name of every morsel of the universe.

"Do you want Charlotte to grow up to be

a Roman orator? Because that's what Quintilian is talking about," Gravit is saying. He is not smirking, like Daphne, but he is not capable of smirking.

"Well, *I* don't want her to be a Roman orator," says Larry, the traitor. "I mean, if that's what she sets her mind on, of course I will support her in her decision, but —"

Very funny, Larry. Betrayed for a bad joke. "Do you want Charlotte to be a bad-flavored vessel?"

"Laurel, really . . ."

"I gave you the book to encourage you to come back," Gravit says gently. Another traitor. "Not to indulge in elitist fear fantasies. There is no passage that says a mother should give up her job, her career, because she is worried about the babysitter's accent."

"It's hardly a career. It's kindergarten."

"*Teaching* is a career," Gravit says, somber with dignity. "More than a career. It's a vocation."

"It's not like you'll never see Charlotte," says the worst traitor of all, Daphne. "You'll be home in the afternoon. Isn't that why mothers become teachers in the first place?"

"It's a *vocation,*" Gravit insists. "A vocation."

"The afternoon? By then the primitive

whiteness of the wool will be dyed."

"Whiteness?" they all cry. "Aha!"

Then there is an embarrassed silence. Because this, Laurel realizes, has been the subtext for them, the awful, reeking subtext.

The primitive whiteness of fucking wool? Good god. They have badgered her and badgered her, and she has exploded into a first-century Roman racist.

Mrs. Gravit is politely yammering, filling the vacuum. "The stuffing is just delicious. I'd love to get the recipe."

Laurel puts her head in her hands. Why can't they understand? Being with Charlotte is not doing nothing. It is doing everything. It *is* everything. It's not the accent of the words, it's being there to hear the words, to hear Charlotte pulling the world toward her, word by word. Laurel wants to be home not to protect Charlotte's speech, but to listen to her speak it, to listen to her, to listen.

"It's not the accent," she says.

She thinks of all the babysitters' accents in the park, a great jumble of laughing and singing and cooing at fussy babies, cajoling and bribing of tired, disobedient toddlers. She wants to sit in the park with Charlotte and listen to this music bestowed on the English language forever. She wants to listen to Charlotte join in. "I just said that about accents because Quintilian said it. And all of you think it's selfish and weak to be a stay-at-home mother."

A general murmur — no, no of course not, murmur murmur, we just want what's best, murmur murmur . . .

"It's not the accent. It's language. The birth of language."

They have stopped laughing, at least. Larry pours her more wine. Daphne flips through the volume of Quintilian.

"It's not the accent or what a babysitter will say to Charlotte," Laurel says. "It's what I'll miss. I don't want to miss it. I don't have to miss it. I just want to be with my daughter. That's all. It's not that complicated."

"Well, maybe you'll come back next year," Gravit says, returning to his meal. "But I do think you should leave poor old Quintilian out of it."

MO'THER. *n.s.* [*moðon,* Saxon; *moder,*
Danish; *moeder,* Dutch.] 2. That which
has produced any thing.
— *A Dictionary of the English Language*
by Samuel Johnson

The first year that Laurel stayed home, she
read nothing, rarely watched television, and
saw virtually no one. Even her phone calls
with her sister were neglected in the new
world of Charlotte, the baby.

"You can never talk," Daphne said. "We're
always interrupted. I have no time, either,
you know."

"I know. It's chaos. I'm sorry. Maybe she
wants to be fed. I'll call you later."

But later, Charlotte would need a diaper
change. Or all her miniature pieces of
laundry would need to be washed and dried
and folded. Or Laurel would need to go to

228

the market to buy bananas.

On each excursion to the butcher or the bakery, Laurel rolled the carriage through the streets like a stranger in an even stranger land, detached from the noise and the energy, and she felt both resentful and grateful that the outer world had so little to do with her and her child.

"It's almost idyllic, to be so isolated," she told Larry. "Or mythic. Epic? Biblical?"

"You forgot Shakespearean and operatic."

"No, not twisted enough for Shakespeare, not broad enough for opera. Just overwhelming and otherworldly and quotidian."

She was happy enough, however, to find a playgroup for her daughter when Charlotte was two — the idyll was becoming exhausting. A few hours to herself — yes, that would do nicely. A few more hours when preschool started next year? Well, yes, even better. Did Laurel stay in her daughter's classroom just a bit longer in the morning than she needed to, just to make sure Charlotte was settled and happy? Perhaps. Did she wait impatiently at dismissal time each afternoon at the door to the school? Probably. It was not an easy transition. But Laurel was, nevertheless, preparing her re-entry into the world.

"By reading *Fowler's Modern English Us-*

age?" Larry asked. He turned the faded blue volume over in his hands, sniffed it, made a face, and gave it back to her.

Laurel put it on her bedside table. The 1967 sixth printing, second edition, revised by Sir Ernest Gowers, a high school graduation gift from Daphne. The dedication neatly printed in their secret twin language translated, simply, as: "Off we go! Love forever, Daphne." It was a book to read randomly, and she began thumbing through it.

"I miss all my words," she said. "I wish I had our old dictionary. The new one is so different."

"The new one? You mean the one that came out in 1961? The one that is a quarter century old?"

"Yes. It's full of newfangled ideas. *Fowler's* is full of oldfangled ideas."

But, reading *Fowler's*, Laurel was surprised at how newfangled some of his old ideas were. Here was a book that she had always thought of as holding language to the highest possible standards, an Edwardian don with a switch and a sorrowful expression. She hadn't looked at the book in years, but *Fowler's* was *Fowler's*, at least *Fowler's* ought to have been *Fowler's*.

She was at first comforted to see that us-

230

ing "ample" with nouns that denote substances of indefinite quantity, like "coal" or "water," rather than restricting it to nouns denoting immaterial or abstract things, like "time" or "courage," was "natural and unexceptionable." She had never said "there is ample water" or "there is ample coal," and she doubted she ever would, partly because there wasn't ample water or ample coal on the planet, and partly because she rarely used the word "ample" except with the word "bosom," and she did not have all that much opportunity for that.

She moved along on the page to "analogy," a long entry, almost an essay, which celebrated the instinctive ingenuity that allows people to make a new word using an analogy to an old word. More than one "book"? "Books"! We know to add an *s* to make it plural because we have already learned that more than one hat, say, is described by the word "hats." Analogy. Daphne was charmed by Fowler's affection — there really seemed no other word for it — for made-up words, though the words were more discovered than created. For if someone created a word that did not fit the correct pattern, it was not a proper word at all. It was the result of a phenomenon Fowler called "faulty word formation." See also Hybrids and Malformations.

"The total poll midway in December was 16,244 so that upward of half the electors were abstentients" — the words of a journalist cited as an example of this transgression, though the journalist himself was not named, perhaps to protect him from angry Fowlerites incensed by his creation of a new word ("abstentients") based on a false analogy with "dissentients." If the anonymous journalist had remembered the Latin verb *abstinere,* a correct "analogy would have led him to 'abstinents.' "

Laurel laughed. How many journalists these days would remember their Latin verbs when trying to come up with a word for more than one voter who did not vote? Daphne? She imagined her sister changing "abstentients" to "abstinents" in *DownTown* and explaining the correction to a writer bug-eyed with rage. In reality, Daphne, even Daphne, would do what Fowler ultimately suggested: she would write "half the voters abstained."

Why did half the voters abstain? Laurel wondered. There was not the faintest indication in Fowler's entry of what the vote was about.

She rubbed her eyes. *Fowler's* was literally musty, which showed how long it had been since she'd cracked open the volume, and her eyes stung.

Dead specimens of unsound analogical bases — they were everywhere, Fowler admitted. "Who thinks of 'chaotic,' 'operatic,' 'dilation,' and 'direful' as malformations? Yet none of them has any right to exist . . ." Except, they do exist, and by existing, "have now all the rights of words regularly made. They have prospered, and none dare call them treason . . ."

Word formation. Even the thought made Laurel uneasy. Here was Fowler, the arbiter, the authority, the last word of the last generation that cared about word usage, implying that distinguished, dignified words were themselves once new words, ungainly words, hobbledehoy words.

She felt vaguely disloyal. To what? To whom? She closed the book, turned off the light, went to sleep.

"I think I have been intellectually understimulated," she said to Larry the next day.

"I can't help you there."

"No. You can't."

They were taking a walk in the late, light summer evening. Charlotte was on Larry's shoulders and kicked her feet on his chest when she wanted him to speed up.

"I was reading Fowler again today. A classic dictionary of usage, and I felt as though I were reading, I don't know, Marx in 1850 or something."

"Revolutionary grammar?"

"Yes!"

"I like Harpo best," Charlotte said. Larry was indoctrinating her with Marx Brothers movies, as well as Charlie Chaplin and Buster Keaton.

"I wonder if there is anyone in the universe who likes Chico or Zeppo the best," Larry said.

Charlotte stopped kicking. "That's sad."

"Charlotte, did you know that everyone makes up new words without even realizing it? Like when a baby learns to say 'book,' and then just from hearing people say 'hat' and then 'hats' when there are more than one, or 'top' and 'tops,' that kind of the thing, the baby thinks, Oh, I'll add an *s* to 'book' because there are a bunch of book so I ought to call them books."

Charlotte said, " 'Books' is not a new word."

"No, but it is for the baby."

"I hate babies."

"I wonder what babies think of you," Larry said.

"Babies don't think! They're *babies.*"

"They stick their heads in gravy and wash

it off with bubble gum and send it to the navy."

Charlotte, who was too young or too sheltered to have heard that particular chant, became quiet and thoughtful.

Laurel was thinking, We have to be *taught* that "oxen" is plural for "ox," but not that "shoes" is plural for "shoe." We use analogy and learn "shoes" on our own without even knowing we're learning it.

She wished analogy did the work for more things human beings had to learn. Like how to make a pie crust. Or make a living. Perhaps it did. Perhaps analogy was the secret of the universe.

"I think I've discovered the secret of life," she said.

Charlotte looked down at her, drawn briefly by the prospect of a secret, but then saw a pretzel cart and lost interest.

Laurel barely noticed. She was thinking about Fowler, how generous he was. Generous toward all the unconscious word-formers of the world. Generous toward even the hapless journalist he could not help but take to task for his fallible analogy of "abstentients." But mostly, generous toward words themselves. She was touched even by the way he phrased things. "Fallible" word formations, as fallible as the hapless humans who created them. He saw language as if it were living and breathing and muddling through like everyone else.

" 'Chaotic' is a malformation," Laurel said aloud.

But Larry and his rider were already galloping off into the park, leaving Laurel on the corner of Seventy-Eighth Street. She found a bench and sat.

Men of the sixteenth century created the word "chaotic," mistakenly using "eros" as a pattern for "chaos." It was a Frankenstein's monster of a word, Laurel thought affectionately, picturing it lumbering this way and that, coarse black stitches across its square green forehead. The monster waved its arms and stumbled wildly. Chaotically.

Eros as a pattern for chaos — all of Western culture resided somewhere in that formulation. But, wait, wasn't Eros the son of Chaos? How complicated and incestuous and Greek, Aeschylus Greek, the whole argument was becoming in her head.

Children pedaled by on bicycles. The summer sun shone yellow and rich through the maple leaves above her. The city sounds hung in the background, a cloud of sound, of shifting gears and screeching brakes and sirens and horns, while children in a nearby playground made high-pitched children noises and a few birds called out into the din. Laurel watched a starling pick at a discarded ice-cream cone. *We're all malformations,* she told the bird as it sparkled off, iridescent, with its bit of garbage. *A bunch of Darwinian accidents that succeed. Words surviving against the hostile forces of habit and convention!*

"Sorry we took so long," Larry said. Charlotte was by his side now, her hand in his. "The horse got tired and we had to dismount and walk back."

"What did you do while we were gone, Mommy?"

"I talked to a bird."

"Did it talk back?"

"No, it just listened."

"Then what's the point?" Charlotte said, and she gave an exaggerated sigh, something she must have learned from a TV show, Laurel thought.

Over the next few weeks, Larry was polite when she mentioned Fowler, Charlotte less so. But even at the risk, the certainty, of exasperating her family, Laurel found she could not resist the faded blue volume.

"It's like pornography," she told Larry. "The more you read it, the more you need to read it. Or so I've heard."

Fowler, gallant and chivalrous, calling for the rescue of words that were "cruelly used"! As if they were running into the fog, shivering on the London streets, clutching pitifully at their thin shawls.

She had to call Daphne. No one else could share her excitement.

"Do you realize," she said to Daphne, "that 'as well as' is a conjunction and not a preposition? So you have to say, 'You were there as well as I,' not 'as well as me'? Fowler swoops in to rescue 'as well as' from prepositionism . . ."

"Prepositionism?" Daphne laughed.

"It's a faulty analogy. My own. But seriously, I don't think I would say, 'You were there as well as I' or 'You were there as well as me.' Would you? I would just say, 'We were both there.' "

"Which would probably be the truth," Daphne said. "In matching outfits."

"Fowler's very protective of words. Like you. But on the other hand, he's also very . . ." Laurel paused. She had been about to say, *He's also very open-minded. And gentle. And gracious.*

"What? Very what?"

"Oh, well, funny. Also like you."

"Thank you, but of course that's bullshit

238

about 'as well as' not being a preposition. Fowler is so inconsistent. You really can't rely on him, Laurel."

The tone was familiar to Laurel. It was a pecking-order tone, a tone that had once been her exclusive right. When had the rank of Older (therefore superior) Sister been degraded to Hobbyist and Housewife? When had Younger (Adoring of Older) Sister become Distinguished Language Columnist? When had the ranks been so drastically reorganized? Perhaps when she had become a housewife and Daphne had become a language columnist.

"In the future," Daphne was saying, "stick to *The Chicago Manual of Style.*"

Unencumbered by a baby and the joyful obligations of motherhood, Daphne had prospered over the last few years.

"I work twenty-four hours a day," she said on one of her rare visits uptown. "Michael, too."

Charlotte, who had just learned that a day had twenty-four hours, looked at her skeptically.

But Daphne did work long hours. And she was getting more and more recognition for her work. The People's Pedant had become so popular that *DownTown* ran it every week. She was asked to go on the local public radio station to discuss a change in the New York City curriculum. She was asked to speak at fund-raising library luncheons. She gave talks in Philadelphia and Boston.

"And boy, does she let you know it," Laurel said one night to Larry.

"Do you want to speak in Philadelphia?" Larry asked.

"No. But I know just as much about language as she does. You know what word I heard her use the other day? My least favorite word: 'loser.' She said someone was a loser. I hate that word. The world is not a competition."

Larry rolled over, closer to her in the bed, put an arm around her. He was half asleep, which he thought was half the right way to be at four in the morning. "I'm sorry you're upset," he said.

"I'm not upset."

You're not competitive, either, he thought, laughing to himself. Not one bit.

"I know she thinks I'm a loser."

"No, I'm sure she —"

"No, she does. I know she does. *I* feel like I've won the lottery, though."

"The Charlottery."

There was a small, satisfied laugh and he

felt the tension leave her. She was asleep.

He got up and sat in Charlotte's room, watching her sleep. Daphne was all right. Charlotte loved her. And he had never had as good a friend as Michael. They played tennis every week, in Riverside Park when it was warm, beneath a big bubble on the East Side when it was not. And they sailed in the summer when the two families descended on Larry's parents at the house in Maine. They were even thinking of getting a little sailboat together. Michael said there was a marina in Brooklyn, far, far out, near Floyd Bennett Field. Larry had never heard of Floyd Bennett Field, but the idea of being able to sail in New York City — well, it was just the kind of idea Michael would have, just the kind of idea Larry would never have, and just another reason that he was so happy to have Michael as a friend. He and Michael were as close as ever, closer, but the two sisters, together, were sometimes . . . he tried to think of the right word. "Childish"! That was the word.

FAR'DEL. *n.s.* [*fardello,* Italian; *fardeau,* Fr.] A bundle; a little pack.
— *A Dictionary of the English Language*
by Samuel Johnson

"This is hell, nor are we out of it." The writer of that sentence was referring to the political situation, and Daphne could not but agree. Even so, it was not the degradation of American ideals that caused her to sputter now as she circled the sentence. It was the use of the word "nor." Daphne jotted down a few notes on a pad, then began writing.

As the People's Pedant, Daphne had perfected a gentle dry tone that was just this side of condescension. She no longer needed to fill her column with words like "fuck" and "shit" and "douchebag" to maintain her credibility. She had only to point out the vagaries of other writers' choices. In the elevator bringing her copy in to the *Times,* she fought off the nagging sense that someone in that building might discover what a feeble, ignorant fraud she was. She fought off the simultaneous feeling of resentment that her new colleagues had yet to recognize her seriousness and brilliance and to therefore resent her back. She fought off the vertigo that had begun the day before.

She was a guest columnist for the most important newspaper in the country while the real language columnist took time off to write a book. And she was pretty sure she was pregnant.

Her editor at the *Times,* a white-haired man of late middle age who sported red suspenders, a cloud of cologne, and the stub of an unlit cigar, made her feel even younger and less important. He was indifferent to most of what she wrote, having been a city reporter before winding up as an editor in the backwater of non-news weekly columns. But he chuckled at this piece, which featured a grammatical faux pas by one of his old rivals.

Daphne tried not to feel as pleased as she did at his approval or as nauseated by his scents. The nausea she thought she understood, but why this breathless, loyal-canine need for an old journalist's praise? It was undignified; it was girlish; it was unprofessional.

And he could sniff out her gratification through his own fumes of Old Spice and tobacco smoke.

"Good girl," he said, patting her head fondly.

By the time the baby was born, she was no longer a guest columnist at the *Times*. She was a regular columnist there. At the newspaper of record, for heaven's sake. A column that ran every other week. And, as if that weren't enough recognition and opportunity from the gods on high, she had a book in the works.

Having so much work to do was essential, she thought, because babies distort the mind. They tire you out and hypnotize you and trick you into superhuman efforts and sleep deprivation that wear you down even more until you are completely under their tiny thumbs and praying to remain there.

"It's a cult," she said to Michael.

The baby lay between them in bed beside the cat.

"Our spiritual leader," he said.

They stared at her for a long time.

"Prudence," Daphne said to the baby.

Daphne loved the name Prudence. She loved that it was a word. It had been Michael's mother's name.

She apologized to her sister for ever doubting the sanctity of babies.

"I was blind but now I see," she said to Laurel one glorious, sunny morning.

Laurel was helping her bump the baby carriage down the steps. Why Michael and her sister had taken an apartment on the third floor of a brownstone when they had so much to drag up and down, she would never understand.

"It's on Charles Street, and it's rent-stabilized," Daphne said. "How many times do I have to explain? Do you know how hard that is to find?"

"But with this carriage . . ."

"We love the carriage, don't we, Prudence? We wouldn't be seen without it." She stopped to say hello to another young woman pushing a baby carriage with one hand and holding the leash of two large collies in the other. "That's my neighbor, Lydia. And that guy over there, going up the steps? He's a weird old shrink. And his daughter is a lesbian named Phoebe and they fight whenever she comes to see him. They leave the windows open and everyone can hear."

Laurel watched the old man struggle to put his key in the lock. Daphne waved to him but he didn't see.

"I love this neighborhood," Daphne said.

"So, worth the steps?"

"God, yes."

Daphne maneuvered the pram into an infinitesimal café and sat down with a grunt of satisfaction. "The best latte here."

Laurel thought of the place they used to go, dark and spacious and dusty. This café, called Café Caffe, was small, sleek, and immaculate. White walls, white tables and chairs, white floors, even. A simple arrangement of yellow miniature roses on each of the six tables.

"It's very cheerful here," she said. "You didn't want to go to the Peacock?"

"For old times' sake? But they have really good croissants here."

"Well, I'm just so happy to see you," Laurel said. "And Prudence, too, of course." Laurel was so happy to be out of her neighborhood, talking to an adult, that they could have met at the women's prison, as far as she was concerned.

Daphne stared down at Prudence, who slept peacefully in the enormous navy blue perambulator. "Thank you again for the carriage. Prudence loves it, don't you, Pru?

And I love to say 'perambulator.' "

"Charlotte outgrew it after about two months. All the baby apparatus . . . you obsess about it and then a few weeks later it's useless."

Her sister said nothing. She was gazing worshipfully into the deep perambulator cave. Laurel had been overjoyed to get it out of their storage space. It was enormous and now took up all the room between their table in the front of the narrow café and the wall, which was also the only way to or from the other tables.

"Maybe you should move her," Laurel said.

"In Iceland they leave carriages outside of shops. Can you imagine?" She reached into her diaper bag and pulled out the Sunday *New York Times,* handing Laurel the bulk of it.

"Here it is," she said after flipping through the one section she kept. She began to read.

Is she reading her own column? Laurel wondered. She is.

Daphne nodded in agreement with herself a few times.

"Okay," she murmured. "Mmm-hmm. Not bad, not bad . . ."

"You're reading your own column?"

"Well, someone has to," Daphne said

cheerfully.

Everyone does, Laurel thought. Everyone I know. But she didn't say it. She said, "Let me see it when you're done."

The quiet of the chic café was suddenly rent by a high-pitched scream originating in the depths of the perambulator. Daphne smiled. "Some lungs," she said proudly.

"Maybe it's time to go."

Daphne reached in for Prudence, held her against her shoulder, banging on her back, spilling her coffee with her elbow. With one hand she mopped up the mess using the crumpled pages that contained her column. "Good for something, anyway," she said with what Laurel considered false modesty.

False modesty was a form of showing off that Laurel didn't have access to much anymore. She resented how easily it came to her sister.

"Just gas," Daphne was saying over the baby's screams. "Don't worry."

"I'm not worried about her, Daphne. It's everyone else in the café."

"Oh, them." Daphne rolled her eyes.

"You know, for someone who judges others so harshly, you're amazingly easy on yourself."

"I don't judge. I discriminate between right and wrong."

A woman tried to make her way past the perambulator. "Excuse me," she said. "Excuse me."

"Perfectly okay. Go right ahead," Daphne said magnanimously as the woman desperately pushed a table out of the way.

"You're lucky you work at home." Laurel tried to keep the envy out of her voice.

"I am a professional scold, and I like it."

"You were born for the job."

Daphne smiled in a bland, complacent way. "That's just what Michael says! Anyway, no one's stopping you from doing anything, Laurel."

"I'm tired of scolding people, though."

"Really? I feel like I'm just getting started. Not *you*," she told Prudence, who was now asleep on her shoulder. "Just the barbarians at the gate."

They walked to the Bleecker Street Playground and sat side by side in the sun, the carriage aimed so that Prudence was in the shade. They watched a little girl carefully poke apart a little boy's sandcastle with a stick.

"Look how methodical she is," Daphne said.

"I think the other kid is about to cry."

"They're playing, that's all."

But a young woman had already moved

in, lifting the girl from the sandbox and apologizing to the little boy, whose lower lip was indeed trembling.

The little girl seemed good-natured enough, and after throwing her stick at the little boy followed her mother to the swings, where she allowed herself to be pushed for the next half hour. Daphne watched them with satisfaction long after Laurel had headed back uptown. She stretched out her legs and eavesdropped on a man next to her who kept ending his sentences with "you know," sometimes as statement, sometimes as a question.

Yes, Daphne thought, closing her eyes, absorbing the sun and the child noises and the sounds of traffic and a dog whining and another dog barking and a distant siren. I think I do know. And that will make a decent little column.

On the subway going home, Laurel looked around, careless about making eye contact, protected by sunglasses. It had not been the sisterly coffee she had imagined, but so few things were what one imagined. In her bag, wrapped in a napkin, there was a croissant she'd gotten for Larry. She broke off a piece and ate it, then another. Daphne was right: the croissant was delicious. She knew Larry would understand though. Really, there was no need to mention the croissant at all. Why tantalize him with something that no longer existed?

When she got home, Larry was peeling off his sweaty clothes in the bedroom after tennis with Michael.

"Charlotte's in her room playing with some new doll my parents gave her," he said. "You just missed them."

He picked up his clothes from the floor and put them neatly in the hamper. Laurel watched him closely.

"What?"

"I still can't believe you do that."

"What?"

"You put your clothes in the hamper. When I lived with Daphne, she would just drop her clothes and leave them like, well, like droppings."

"Kind of like you?"

She laughed. "Listen, I think I may want to go back to teaching this year. What do you think?"

"I think that's great," he said. "I had a feeling you would."

"You did? Why?"

Oh, I don't know. Because you're reading an old grammar book and saying that Daphne thinks you're a loser. He said nothing, closed the bathroom door partway, and got into the shower.

"I don't want to be Charlotte's teacher, though," she yelled through the crack.

"Why?" Charlotte said. She had snuck up on Laurel, as she often did.

"Because the other children would be jealous. I'd make you sit on my lap and I'd smother you in kisses and I'd call you Charchar and Choo-choo."

Charlotte nodded in sober agreement. She said, "Yes, and then I might kick you."

"That's my girl."

Gravit's solution for the mother/daughter kindergarten dilemma was that Laurel should teach sixth grade. He needed a sixth-grade English teacher.

"How can I teach sixth grade? I'm not qualified. I barely made it through kindergarten.

"Come on board and fill old Mrs. Turner's shoes."

The thought of old Mrs. Turner's shoes made the whole idea even less appealing.

"What are Mrs. Turner's shoes like?" Larry asked.

"I've never noticed. I'm sure they're sensible. She's sensible. Or she was until she got so . . ."

"Nonsensible?" Larry said. "So, what, she switched to Manolo Blahnik?"

Larry was covering for her. How sweet of him. She needed to think. She poured more wine for all of them. She got the chicken marbella out of the oven. Olives, prunes, capers. Her father once told her that capers were fish eyes, and she had believed him for years. You have to be so careful what you say to children. They can be so literal-minded. How could she possibly cope with a class of sixth-graders, practically adolescents, literal-mindedly challenging every word she uttered? She couldn't trick them by singing, the way she had the little ones in kindergarten.

"I'm so sorry Pamela couldn't make it," Larry was saying.

"Yes, so am I. But she's gone."

"Where to?"

"Gone to her mother's," Gravit said in a melancholy voice.

"She was at her mother's the first time we had you to dinner," Laurel said. "Daphne and I, remember? When you brought us Bunny the cat in your briefcase instead of wine. Daphne was certain his wife had left him that night," she said to Larry. "But Pamela had just gone to visit her family."

Gravit's chin was shiny with oil from the

chicken. Laurel wished Pamela were there to mop him up. He was drinking an awful lot, too. He tipped his glass back to get the last few drops, then held the glass out to Laurel, tapped it for more.

"Now she really has," he said.

"Has what?" Laurel poured him another glass, not as full as the last three.

He frowned at the glass, reached across the table, and took the bottle. "Left me."

"Business trip?" Larry asked. He looked at Laurel, the bottle, back at Laurel, and opened his eyes wide in a signal of alarm. "Where to?"

A shrug from Gravit. "Away. Gone. Gone away." A sigh. A tear.

"Hey, whoa," Laurel said. She handed Gravit the clean napkin from his wife's empty place. "Pamela *left you* left you? As in left you?"

She poured Gravit another glass in a sort of haze. The subject of the conversation had molted so suddenly, and what was left? That plucked, naked creature: Mr. Gravit. But the thought of Gravit naked was not a felicitous one and she pushed it from her mind. She looked at him, clothed in his Gravit clothes, the front of his necktie higher than the back, the tag showing. A collar stay that had not stayed and poked out from one bent wing of his frayed shirt collar. Ink stain in his breast pocket. A bright Bugs Bunny bandage on his thumb. The end of his watchband was not in its keeper and flopped as he wiped his eyes with the napkin. He was such a hapless thing. How could Pamela abandon such a man, an eternally flightless nestling?

Yet he functions perfectly well in the world, Laurel reminded herself. He'd held on to his well-paying, prestigious — to the extent there was any pay or prestige in education — position for years, and the school had prospered under his guidance. He amused the parents. He was their Mr. Chips and it suited them to patronize him rather than question him, which allowed him to do exactly what he wanted to do, which made the school better and better. He was a kind of benevolent, passive-aggressive tyrant, she realized, a poorly dressed, highly articulate Zen willow that bends in the wind and never breaks the way the brittle trees around it do. Never breaks but also soaks up all the good sunlight and the rain and all the rich soil, and she suddenly imagined Pamela's life. But the willow gives back refreshing shade, she quickly reminded herself. She moved to the chair next to him and put her arm around his shoulders. "I'm so sorry," she said.

"I don't think she'll be back. She's always come back before. But I think she's had it. Because imagine living with me," he continued. "It can't have been easy."

"Well, no," Laurel began.

"But *no one* is easy to live with," Larry said quickly. "Not me. Right, Laurel?"

"Well, you are pretty easy to live with," she said, then caught his eye and said, "I mean, no, no, you're impossible."

"She *might* come back, you know," Gravit said, looking up from his glass. "She always has before," he repeated. "In the past. She has come back. But not this time, no, I can tell. Why would she? Unless she changes her mind." He sighed. "She has, you know." More sighs. More wine. "In the past."

"Right," Larry said. "That's right."

" 'Let grief convert to anger!' " Gravit banged his fist on the table. He was truly drunk now, his speech slow and heavy. "Or not. I'll just go on as before. One day much like another. Not like Macbeth at all. A lonely dinner at a dimly lit diner. Alone. A lonely —"

"How is Miranda taking it?"

"Miranda? The stormy child swept up in the storm. Miranda. She suffers with those she sees suffer . . ." He went on, quoting

Shakespeare and Horace and, once, Cole Porter, until abruptly he stopped, facedown on the table, like a toy that had run out of batteries.

"Should we put him in a cab?" Larry asked.

"But where can we send him? Home? What if Pamela left but also kicked him out of the house? Or something. I don't know. And how would he even get in the door, in his state?"

They stood over him and watched him for a few silent moments. Then Laurel poked his shoulder. "Are you there, Gravit, it's me Laurel."

"Excellent book," he murmured. "Excellent woman, Judy Blume. Fucking parents, fucking ignoramuses . . ."

With some patience, difficulty, and firm words, they were able to help Mr. Gravit, headmaster, onto the couch and cover him with a blanket.

"Well," Laurel said as they got into their own bed. "I guess this means I'll be teaching sixth grade next year, doesn't it?"

"I think you might have to. As a humanitarian act. You can't really leave Askew in the lurch now. Too many lurches at one time."

Charlotte was delighted to find Mr. Gravit

on the couch in the morning. She brushed his scanty hair as if he were a huge doll.

It did not take Laurel long to adjust to sixth grade. The old, pleasant feeling of Teacher had washed over her as soon as she walked into the classroom: she was a shepherd, a sheepdog, a shrink, a referee, a prophet, a friend. The children, awkwardly approaching the supreme awkwardness of adolescence, sucked on their new braces and smelled like the fruity soaps from the chain of shops that had overtaken her neighborhood hardware store, but there was an arrogance still softened by innocence, which she found irresistible.

Gravit was a little smug about her easy transition to sixth grade. But smug, as an emotion, was a step up from his general sadness, and Laurel did not mind. He spent a fair amount of time at the apartment now that he'd been kicked out of his house.

"Just thought I'd drop by for a minute. I've brought you a book," he said on each visit. Then he would settle himself on the sofa. The books were often in Latin, old volumes from the library he was disassembling.

"Now, this book," he said one Saturday afternoon, "could be very helpful. It was revolutionary in its time. It would have been, at any rate, if more people had read it."

"When was its time?"

"Nineteen twenty-six."

He placed the green clothbound book in her hands, tenderly.

"The study was begun in 1926, but the war came along, you know. One of my professors studied with the author at Michigan. He gave this book to me. And now I give it to you."

American English Grammar, English Monograph No.10, National Council of Teachers of English by Charles Carpenter Fries.

"Sexy title."

"He was interested in real, spoken language rather than formal, written language."

"Hence the sexy, colloquial title," Laurel said, thinking, *English as She Is Spoke!* "But why is spoken language more real than written? Written lasts longer. Spoken English is so . . . ephemeral."

"So is life," Gravit said. And marriage, he was obviously thinking.

"Yes, but come on, Gravit, that's exactly why written language is so important, good language in books, because it's not ephemeral."

But Gravit was no longer listening. He was

examining the ads for apartment rentals in *The New York Times.* "Laurel!" he cried out. "There is a one-bedroom across the street from my house. I will be able to wave at Miranda!"

"Wave *to* Miranda, I hope."

"We're talking about Miranda, Laurel. Wave *at.*"

Laurel pictured the headmaster in his disheveled pajamas raising a dejected hand hopefully behind an unwashed windowpane. Across the street, his thirteen-year-old daughter, her hair animal-wild, her pink sweatshirt and leopard leggings flashing past the window of the brownstone her parents had bought so many years ago when no one in their right mind wanted a brownstone on that particular street, without a glance outside. Which one was ephemeral, she wondered: the waver or the wavee?

" 'Ephemeral' is a pretty word, isn't it? It sounds like a pretty girl's name. How is Miranda, by the way?"

"Forceful." And he snapped the newspaper open in front of his face the way her father used to do when he did not want to discuss something.

Out of politeness, Laurel opened the book Gravit had given her. She read aloud: " 'Anxiety concerning the kind of English spoken and written by English people seems to have had its most vigorous early expression in the eighteenth century as an outgrowth of the striving for 'elegance' and especially attending the rise of the commercial middle classes into more prominence socially.' "

Striving for "elegance," she thought. Oh dear. "Striving," she said.

"Yes," Gravit said from behind his newspaper. "I'm afraid so."

" 'The study of grammar was . . . deeply intrenched in the traditional prejudices of the public'," she read. "So proper grammar is nouveau riche?"

Was that what Daphne was fighting for in her columns? Overcompensating, ostentatious social climbers?

"Well, Daphne would not like this guy, that's for sure," she said. "Proper English is just another *vernacular*? A social dialect? A class dialect? I'm not sure I like that, either. I mean, grammar is grammar. Some things are just wrong."

As children, Daphne and Laurel had memorized grammar rules and set them to nursery tunes. If there were no standards, what was left? The man was a nihilist. *English as She Is Spoke,* indeed!

"I suppose he would be called a descrip-

261

tivist now," Gravit said.

"Descriptivists versus prescriptivists? They both sound like brand-X Protestant religions to me." *Ah, yes, I was brought up in a strict prescriptivist family,* she imagined a lapsed prescriptivist saying with a rueful shake of the head, *but I have lost my faith.* She said, "What is the point of describing language with *language?* The whole enterprise is so tautological, it's practically mystical."

"Are you dismissing the entire discipline of linguistics?"

"But for grammar, why not just get the rules right and move forward?" *Rules were there for a reason,* as she often told Charlotte, though when Charlotte demanded to know that reason, Laurel was sometimes reduced to saying, "Because that's the way it's done."

"That is certainly the view of the People's Pedant," Gravit said. "But doesn't her column sometimes make you suspect that language is not very different from fashion or manners? Table manners, for example." *Laurel thought, Gravit is not someone who should be talking about table manners.*

"Using a fish fork," he continued. "Even knowing what a fish fork looks like. That's a sign that you grew up in a certain milieu. In a certain era. In a particular culture."

"Right, but —"

"It's not a sign of virtue or truth."

Laurel imagined the flag of a newly liberated country declaring its dedication to democratic values. Fishforkia!

"But should points of grammar carry so much moral weight?" Gravit said. "All Fries is saying is that using, say, the possessive gerund is not a sign of virtue or of truth. Both the fish fork and the possessive gerund are signs, all right. But they're signs of age, social convention, and class."

Laurel disliked the word "class." It was too easy. It was always the answer to every difficult, unsolvable question. It carried its Marxist intransigence with it like a musty smell.

But too bad, Laurel, she said to herself. Just because you are embarrassed by the months you spent chanting, "Ho, Ho, Ho Chi Minh," in 1968 does not negate the concept of class.

"So that's why people like Daphne's column? Knowing when to say 'continuous' instead of 'continual' sets them off from the masses?"

"Well, partly. Don't you think? Of course, we're all romantic, spiritual beings, too. We all want to transcend contingency in our lives. We are always searching for something universal. Even if it's just rules of grammar. That's another attraction."

"The universality of fish forks," Laurel said.

"Yes, well, you see the problem right there."

LE´SSER. *adj.* A barbarous corruption of
less, formed by the vulgar from the habit
of terminating comparatives in *er;* after-
wards adopted by poets, and then by
writers of prose.
— *A Dictionary of the English Language*
by Samuel Johnson

"The boy no doubt secured the services of some one falsely representing herself as his sister." (78)

Oh dear, thought Laurel. A young soldier with his "sister." I've heard that before — just not as an example of the demise of the inflected genitive in modern English.

How clever of Fries to use letters written to the Department of War. He anticipated corpus linguistics, according to Gravit. The man had no computers at his disposal, no body of recordings of everyday speech. But

265

he realized he did have a corpus of everyday speech. He had letters — letters from people across the country, letters from every county, rural or urban, from every age and every social class. All the letters were sent to the one place that could expect such a flood of missives from such different sorts of Americans — the Department of War.

When most written language was formal, here were examples from people across the country, across social and educational strata, across race and gender and age.

She flipped to a page discussing the use of a plural subject followed by a singular verb. (52): "My children is too small." That made her smile, imagining a woman with her hands on her hips staring at a bunch of stubby children. But the next example brought her up short. "My children is on starvation." The children who were too small were not too small for their mother's vanity. They were too small to have to bear whatever had befallen them. These were the letters of mothers and fathers and sons and daughters and wives and grandparents, the soldiers and their sweethearts and parents and children, the ones who came back and the ones left behind. All united by war.

"But births was not recorded when James

was born."

"The dirt floors requires continual work."

"All my uncles was in the civil war."

"The times is so hard."

The grammatical examples were all like that, sad and unique, because they were pieces of people's lives, scraps of lives on scraps of paper.

"It's like a Woody Guthrie song," she told Larry. "The indefinite pronoun with number distinctive form? It's heartbreaking. And a preterit form used for the past participle in strong verbs? Listen:

" 'My folks may have rote you.'

" 'I hope I haint don any thing rong or rote anything rong in this letter.'

" 'I have broke my health to have a home to live in.'

" 'He was the best boy I ever had and has give me most help.'

" 'He liyed about his self in the army and was took without letting me know any thing about it.'

" 'I wish you would see what has become of my son.'

" 'Everything I have wrote is the truth.' "

Laurel could not get that out of her head: Everything I have wrote is the truth.

"Because that's the point of words, right?

The truth."

"Unless you're lying," Larry said.

In response, because she was angry at his stupid, unfeeling joke, if it was a joke, Laurel loudly directed two lines from the next page at him:

" 'Maybe I hadn't ought to write to you / But I was afraid I would do something I had not ought to do.' "

Then, angry and hurt, she left him in the living room to finish the perfect dry martini in its icy glass with its three olives she had just made him.

He followed her into the kitchen, offering a sip as a gesture of peace. She drank from his glass, more than a sip, but said nothing.

"You're not speaking to me?"

She read from the Fries book: " 'I said he didn't no / What he was doing and he didn't and I have just showing you he didn't.' "

Larry looked at the page. "You changed the pronoun. It says 'she' didn't know what 'she' was doing."

"That, too," Laurel said.

The grammar book haunted her. She often made Larry read strings of the excerpts aloud. She was filled with a vague guilt that got more vague, rather than less, the more she thought about why. She remembered her sister's notebooks, all those words collected like butterflies, pinned to the page. They struck her now as morbid, even tragic. And her own contribution, the careful transcription of definitions from *Webster's New International Dictionary of the English Language,* Second Edition — the words she copied from the dictionary might just as well have been the handsome penmanship of a Victorian vicar inscribing the species of each dead bright-winged lepidopteran.

She tried to talk to Daphne about it once.

"Remember how we used to play with your word collection? We played with the words as if they were toys?"

Daphne laughed. "The collection! 'Oxters'! That was a fun one. You were very dedicated, writing in all the definitions."

She made Laurel's task sound so dowdy.

"And remember your skin collection?" Daphne said.

Laurel had so envied Daphne's little notebooks and pads full of collected words that she had tried to come up with something interesting she could collect. Briefly she had considered collecting peeled sunburned skin, watching to see what happened to it over time. But in the end, the idea of rotting skin in a box, even her pretty jewel box, was too frightening.

"I never actually did it."

"Ah, life, fugacious life."

Laurel told her about the grammar book, about the desire to understand how people really spoke, about the snippets of sadness that would not leave her head, or her heart, once she read them. "It's so sad," she said. "All these people reaching out. Hearing their voices through the grammar."

"You know, you probably react so emotionally because you can picture them as poor and uneducated, and that's because their English is so poor and uneducated. How can they ever succeed in the world and pull themselves out of their poverty if they can't speak proper English? I mean, that's his point, right? He was in education, right?"

"No, that's not his point. His point is, informal English is not wrong, and some of it stems from models older than 'standard' English, and he always puts 'standard' in quotes because there is no standard English, language keeps changing. And to understand language and teach it, you have to know what is actually spoken."

"Oh. One of those."

"London, which was where the movers and shakers of the fourteenth and fifteenth century hung out, had a local dialect. If you wanted to sound like you were in the know, like you were one of the power elite, you dropped your Kentish dialect and started speaking in Londonese. Otherwise you sounded like a rube. And that keeps happening. What people call 'standard' English is really just the dialect of the elite."

"Okay, five hundred years later, here we are, Laurel. I have no interest in sounding like a rube. Neither do you. But at least the bad English in this book — and it sounds awful — at least it's in letters from people with hardly any education. What I can't stand is the way that stuff has crept into normal English. You can't even call it Vulgar English the way your guy does. It's become Standard English. Standard. No quotes. It's depressing."

"You're so cold, Daphne. Jesus."

"I have standards, that's all. And I'm sorry, but you're reading me grammatical mistakes from the nineteen-twenties. It's not like it's literature."

Which gave Laurel an idea. Which made Laurel think. Which changed Laurel's life.

LA´TED, *adj.* [from *late:*] Belated; surprised
 by the night.
 — *A Dictionary of the English Language*
 by Samuel Johnson

Personal, tragic fragments of family dramas,
economic hardship, physical disaster and
decline. The genitive of possession trans-
forms itself into dispossession: *The boy's
father is in the insane asylum; I am forced
from my mothers by my stepfather.*
 Genitive pronouns become glimpses of the
most intense need: *I am crippled in my limbs.
Get this boy back or break up my home. Help
Save Our Crops. He is my youngest boy.*
Suggestive, eloquent, incomplete, full. The
grammar fades almost entirely and Laurel
no longer sees the words, she hears the
voices of the letters calling out. These are
splinters of poetry.

This was his second time to leave home.
I am not able to pay his way here to
    assist me in my last days.
He lied about his age on account of his
    minority.
5 yr's his limit to live.
His pictures show that he is very thin.

Laurel spends time at the library, the main branch on Fifth Avenue, the cathedral of words. At a long wooden table she reads an essay by Richard Rorty in the *London Review of Books*. (She has begun to read literary quarterlies, too, little magazines of poetry and stories.) The essay is about Freud and Nietzsche and Hegel and Plato and all of Western thought, and it begins with a poem by Philip Larkin, and Laurel cannot properly explain it to Larry when she gets home, but she feels extravagantly alive when she reads it, as if the gods had breathed life into her: inspired, literally. She has written down one sentence: "We are doomed to spend our conscious lives trying to escape from contingency rather than, like the strong poet, acknowledging and appropriating contingency."

And Laurel begins to write.

"Write about what you know," Larry says. "Isn't that what they tell you?"

But Laurel does not write about what she knows. She writes about what others knew, what others said, in the phrases of mothers and fathers and daughters and sons and widows and wives, phrases that improbably survive, like lines of Sappho, from letters collected by the Department of War. "He ran off and joined the army to keep out of trouble and he had to drink to keep from going crazy . . . so he lied to enlist . . . I had to borrow to get him home . . . his pay is not sufficient to properly care for me . . . he does not make enough to properly support me and his mother . . . I am writing to assure you I desire to arrange my affairs."

Laurel reads the lines again and again. "I kneed him, I am 50 years old, with 5 little ones to support, with bothe knees all to pieces with rheumatism . . ." The voices became softer, sadder. "After a Mother & Father suffer to raise a Boy . . . I am asking for your help to locate my son . . . Please leave my son come home . . . I hate to let it go so bad . . . Help save our crops and help rase the twoo little boys . . ."

The misspellings strike her as painfully eloquent, not mistakes at all, but cries of the heart, documentation of upheaval in a family, in a social order.

"Say it soft and it's almost like singing,"

she says to Daphne.

But Daphne does not hear the singing. She hears condescension and nostalgia from Laurel. She hears Marie Antoinette parading around in a peasant dress. She hears sentimentality. She hears her sister lost in a folly of maudlin romance.

"Leonard Bernstein it ain't."

Laurel is not discouraged. She is simply secretive now. She quits her job. She goes back to the public library on Fifth Avenue and reads and writes. She reads this example of what Charles Fries calls the subjective genitive: " 'Knowing that we couldn't get along without the Boys help' (context shows that Boys is singular — a son)."

And she writes a crude poem:

The Boys
In war, a mother writes a letter
or a father
or the war itself writes the letter,
"knowing
that we couldn't get along
without the Boys help."
Without the Boys.
Without the Boys help
we couldn't get along,
You know that as well as we do.

In war
(context shows that
Boys
is singular —
a son)

But she is on her way. She appropriates
contingency. The voices call out the way
poetry calls out, quietly, insistently, demanding to be heard not just by Laurel but by
others, too. The voices in the grammar book
speak to each other and to her, and now
they will speak to whoever reads what she
has written.

This is what words do, she realizes. They
call out from the page and force you to
listen. No, they allow you to listen.

Laurel's poems of appropriation become
whole worlds of appropriation. *The boy's
father is in an insane asylum; I want you to
get this very plain; I never had occasion to
use Geometry* — Laurel listens to the voices
of the grammar ghosts and hears their plain-
tive fragments as stories. *Help take care of
him, if you will kindly think of me, I am very
much in need of him at home, I am now asking of you, there is three of us.*

The acknowledgment and appropriation
and writing take time. Years. Five years pass.
One of her stories of appropriation is

printed in a little magazine, and then another in another little magazine. Five more years pass. Her daughter is a teenager. Her husband is terrified of his teenage daughter. Laurel writes a story with a title taken from one of the lines in Charles Fries's book — "It Takes 6 Days for a Letter to Get to New York" — and the story is printed in *The New Yorker. The Grammar Ghosts,* a collection of stories, is published. Her work is called "sampling" and is compared to hip-hop. And her sister is not speaking to her.

Michael and Daphne closed the door on their departing guests with a sigh of relief. He put his arm around Daphne and held her close to him. He was always relieved when he and Daphne were alone again. Daphne was tagged as the dramatic member of the family, but he had been with her long enough now to see that the charged emotion she was supposed to carry was usually tossed aside as soon as she was away from them. Particularly Laurel. Or any mention of Laurel. Someone had mentioned Laurel at dinner.

"I'm really upset," Daphne said.

"I thought the lamb was delicious. And if someone doesn't say they're a vegetarian ahead of time, how are you supposed to know? Angie got plenty of salad. And potatoes."

"I don't mean the goddamn lamb, and you know it."

He said nothing. Their friends had mentioned reading a story by Laurel in *Harper's Magazine.*

"No one reads *Harper's,* anyway," Daphne said.

Michael blocked a sigh, but she caught it.

"Well, she's ridiculous, you know she is, Michael. I mean, let's start with the nose. I'm sorry, but what *was* that about? I should ask Uncle Don. Does she hate her face so much, which by the way is my face, that she had to turn it into a whole other face?"

Michael did not say, *It's not your face, Daphne.* He did not say, *It's her nose to do with as she pleases.* He did not say, *The surgeon did a beautiful job, it looks completely natural and not all that different.* He did not say that was over a decade ago. He had said all of it so many times before.

"And now Charlotte looks more like me than she looks like Laurel. So I guess that backfired."

Michael began clearing the table. It was

pretty rude of Angie, he thought, not to give them a vegetarian warning.

"And now she's a poet?" Daphne said, following him from dining room to kitchen. "A short-story writer? It's cut-and-paste, Michael. Plagiarism, really, when you think about it, which I don't, but god."

He was glad, actually, that the meat they had served was lamb. The only thing better would have been veal. That'll show you, Angie. He wondered if Angie mentioned the story by Laurel as revenge for the slaughtered little lamb.

"You know what she called me?" Daphne said.

"You hardly even speak to her. You two are impossible. Do I have to start seeing Larry on the sly?"

"The last time we spoke she called me a prescriptivist! You know what that is? A person who cares about proper language usage. A person who cares about the rules of grammar."

"But you do care about that. That's what you write about. What's wrong with that?"

"Nothing. But she says it the way you say a dirty word. Or . . . or 'Nazi.' Because she's been reading all this stuff about education, and this crap about how we can only describe what is being said, and whatever is being said is what is right. English is not Latin, she says. All your rules are imposed on English. All your rules were invented in the seventeenth century to make English seem more like Latin. Or, even worse, French! All *my* rules, she says! As if rules weren't rules but just some . . . some fetish of mine! Laurel the Descriptivist! It's ridiculous! She didn't want Charlotte to have a babysitter because she was worried about her speaking with a, let's face it, lower-class accent! And now she's telling me I'm narrow-minded because I think using 'they' in the singular is wrong? And she gets her nose fixed so she won't look Jewish? So she can follow the Barbie-doll rule of nasal beauty conformity? With her WASP husband? Well, who's the real prescriptivist? Who's the Nazi now?"

Michael rinsed dish after dish and placed them in the dishwasher. Daphne rearranged each one. Wasn't I just remarking to myself that she was not really the theatrical loon her family makes her out to be? he thought.

She began to shake him. "I know what you're thinking," she said, "so just spit it out!"

"Okay, this is what I'm thinking: she's your sister."

280

Daphne removed her hands from his shoulders. "The story of my fucking life."

OBERRA´TION. *n.s.* [from *oberro,* Latin.]
The act of wandering about.
— *A Dictionary of the English Language*
by Samuel Johnson

There was something wayward in the twins' relationship now, a devious shift Sally sensed but could not catch in the act. For a long time before the Rift, as the often odious and occasionally prescient Don had called it, had separated them completely, it unraveled gradually, like a tear in a sweater. Sally recognized it before she was willing to. The family brunch in honor of the pending first grandchild, which Daphne refused to attend, yes, that should have been a sign, thank you hindsight, useless as always. Then, with Daphne's move to Brooklyn, well, you had to be blind not to notice. Their excuses were always sensible — the subway took forever, a cab was unthinkably expensive, there was always something one or the other of them had to do — but Sally knew the distance between the twins was not just geographical. She could feel it; it disturbed her to think of the girls separated from each other. She had repeatedly tried to lure them out to Larchmont together, but there was always some barrier — school, work, after-school, and, Mom, frankly, you know, *life.*

"Daphne writes a weekly column, Mom," Laurel had said when Sally first complained to her. "She's collecting her columns into a book *and* she's collaborating with Michael on a book about how doctors and patients miscommunicate. Prudence is practically a baby. Daphne's *busy.*"

"Do you know how hard teachers work?" Daphne said when Sally complained, in turn, to her. "The planning and correcting and the reports. The conferences. It never ends. And Charlotte needs help with her homework. And she goes to fencing class and dance class and the piano teacher. Laurel is *busy.*"

At first it reassured Sally when each daughter stood up for the other. She had still thought of them as a unit, two sides leaning in, propping up the whole, a single edifice in two parts. But in time their excuses seemed not like a defense of the other one, but a defense against the other one.

"Just don't forget your sister's birthday," she told Laurel, who laughed obligingly.

"Just don't forget your sister's birthday," she said to Daphne, who laughed in just the same way.

Okay, girls, the joke is on you, Sally thought irritably when she'd hung up the phone that day. And she began planning a big birthday party for herself, one neither of them would dare miss.

This was years ago, five, six — no, eight years ago. Arthur was still alive. Laurel had not published anything yet.

Daphne had arrived first, breathless with importance. And why not? Several of Sally's friends headed straight for Daphne to offer compliments on her last column and offer suggestions for future columns, some slang word they objected to or an offensive neologism. Sally watched her daughter smile uncertainly, nod uncertainly, take Michael's hand, and extricate herself from them, uncertainly.

She knew Daphne was still reeling from her good fortune, that she was both proud and embarrassed, relishing what she was not quite sure she deserved. She knew because Daphne told her. When Sally went to Park Slope to visit, she and Daphne sometimes sat together in the backyard. Even in winter, beneath the leafless tree under the cold blue sky, they wrapped themselves in blankets and talked and talked — talked in a way they never had before. Those were satisfying days for Sally. She had never gotten enough of either child when they were growing up. She wondered if they had gotten enough of her.

Daphne would sit with her in the Brooklyn backyard, put her head back, and stare at the bare tree and the cloudless sky. She would tell Sally how tired she was, how thrilled, how frightened of losing it all.

Once, just once, Sally had suggested that Daphne worked too hard. "And now with this big house . . ."

Daphne had turned to the house, looked up at the three narrow stories, and said, "Only in New York would this be considered a big house. It has one bathroom." She turned back to her mother. "One bathroom," she said, in a kind of wonder.

Then she asked Sally if she was insufferable, and Sally assured her that she was just as sufferable as she had always been. They had both laughed comfortably, and Sally knew she must not disturb that comfort by asking what had happened with Laurel.

She had shared similar moments with Laurel years before when Charlotte was a baby. There was something about having a child that opened her children to her, their mother. Sally's illness had brought both of them to her side. She treasured the intimacy, though she knew it suggested not just a deeper feeling about motherhood or concern about her health but also a weakening of the intimacy between Daphne and Laurel.

When she first tried to bring up the estrangement with Laurel, then with Daphne, their answers were — comically, Sally thought — identical: "We're not married to each other, Mother."

At the birthday party she gave for herself eight long years ago, Sally had watched Daphne and her admirers, watched Prudence launch herself across the terrace toward the pile of presents, watched Daphne take Michael's hand and, once free of the others, swing it up and down like a happy child. Daphne grinned at her, and Sally grinned back.

What a good idea, she'd thought. I should give myself a party every year.

I didn't know Arthur would die. I didn't know the cancer would come back. If I had known, would I have enjoyed that party more? Or not at all?

All Sally knew was that she had enjoyed it tremendously. Ignorance was blissful that day. And her daughters had been wonderful, so beautiful walking together in the afternoon sunlight, their red hair still fiery and shining. Her grandchildren had played together, little cousins romping on the lawn. Arthur had put his arm around her and called her Old Thing.

Laurel and Daphne had spoken to each other before the party. They were no longer in the habit of talking on the phone every day, or talking very much at all, but they were on good enough terms to discuss what present to get their mother. Should it be something from both of them? Yes, of course it had to be from both of them. Without even having to say it, they knew that would be the real present — the fact that it came from them together as one. A year's worth of monthly spa days? A cashmere sweater? It hardly mattered as long as they both signed the card and presented it together.

When Laurel got to the birthday party, the first person she came upon was Prudence roosting in a pile of wrapping paper and brightly colored tissue.

"Happy birthday!" the little girl said to

Aunt Laurel, looking dazed.

"Happy birthday to you, too!"

"I'm overstimulated!" Prudence said, then waved goodbye and ran off trailing ribbon to follow her big cousin, Charlotte, and Charlotte's au pair, Miranda the Assistant. Laurel and Larry had hired Gravit's daughter as their mother's helper that summer, and she dutifully ran alongside the little girls, explaining a game, its rules technical, complicated, and bountiful.

"She has got to be the world's bossiest au pair," Laurel said.

"Read too much Mary Poppins as a child."

Sally watched her two granddaughters play with the babysitter, that beautiful girl who had been the flower girl. At least my grandchildren are playing nicely with each other, she thought. They ran by her, squealing.

"You naughty children broke the rules," the babysitter was yelling, "and I will catch you and cook you for my dinner!" She ran after them, which made them squeal and laugh more, suddenly turning on her and tackling her to the ground.

"I must really be getting old," Sally whispered to Arthur. "The ruckus! It's like Grand Central Station."

He made a lame joke about it being her

thirty-ninth birthday, did his Jack Benny imitation, and took her wineglass to refill it.

Sally spotted Aunt Beverly approaching. Beverly's husband had died the year before. Looking back now, with Arthur gone, Sally understood Beverly's determination not to let her sorrow slow her down, but at the time it had seemed unnatural and more macabre in its way than widow's weeds.

"Isn't this a cheerful chaos?" Beverly said. Bright, brave Beverly! See how bright and brave I am? She had adopted a perpetual smile — plucky, ghastly. Or so Sally thought at the time. She understood it better later.

"What fun!" bright brave Beverly added.

Sally hugged her and felt how small Beverly had become, a bony, birdlike figure.

But it was Beverly who said, "Sally! You've lost weight! You're all skin and bones," then caught herself with a small gasp. Was she remembering why Sally was thin? Or re-membering to be bright and brave?

"The chemo. It does that."

Beverly's smile wavered, then gathered strength again.

"Modern medicine!" she said.

"Yes. A miracle." And it was. One-breasted like an Amazon and on her way to her second year cancer-free. She smiled back at Beverly. "So many things happen. Yet here we are."

Now they had a real hug. They both cried a little. Then Beverly straightened herself up and marched off.

After Laurel wished her mother a happy birthday and embraced both her parents, exchanging the loud kissing noises her mother and father insisted on making these days — *Mwah! MMMwaHH* — she looked around for Daphne. Instead, here were Uncle Don and Aunt Paula standing together by the makeshift bar. Paula looked contentedly bored, as she often did. Poor Uncle Don was never content, Laurel thought, or bored. How can you be bored when you are so alert to other people's opinions about you? Extreme, if narrow, engagement is constantly required. Takes it out of you.

"A family reunion," she said to them. "Just like the old days. Where's Brian?"

"Up a tree," Don said.

"He's on the beach birding, that's what Don means. He'll be here soon."

"He prefers birds to his own family."

Paula gave Laurel a look as if to say, *Can you blame him?*

"Well, he is an ornithologist, Uncle Don."

"Do you think Brian's gay?" Paula asked. "Don thinks Brian might be gay because he

290

doesn't like football."

"Hey, there's your answer! Gay as a goose."

"I *don't* think he's gay," Don said. "I was just wondering what that might imply."

Laurel let the bartender, an unhappy girl who was probably underage, where on earth had her mother dug her up, pour her two glasses of white wine.

"For Larry," she said to her aunt and uncle, then hurried off to share with him the Uncle Don gossip.

Brian did not see anything of particular interest, but he enjoyed the walk along the beach, and it postponed meeting up with his family. He had come down from Cornell at his parents' insistence: It was his Aunt Sally's big birthday bash, but also they had something important they wanted to tell him. They were getting divorced, they wanted him to be the first to know.

"Okay," he said, not sure if he was surprised or not. "I'm sorry. I want both of you to be happy."

"Please don't tell anyone," his mother said.

Was it a secret divorce? God, they were weird. Weirder and weirder as time went on.

"We're just not ready to announce it," his

father said.

His mother took his father's hand. "Not just yet."

Brian promised he would say nothing, grabbed his binoculars, and headed for the beach. He sat on the sand and watched a few gulls pick through the low-tide rocks. His parents were ridiculous. Dragging him home to make their big announcement, then dragging him to his aunt and uncle's to keep their big announcement a secret. Okay, he was upset. He admitted it. He wasn't that surprised, except that they were so old, but he was upset. What was the point, after so many years? His mother said she had found someone she was more compatible with, a lawyer, a judge actually, Malcolm McManis, a wonderful man, they both said. They were obviously determined to be civilized about it all. But that made it so much weirder. How did they not see that? He wondered how long it would take his father to find someone and how old she would be. Probably his age. He felt a pang of sadness at the uselessness of everything. Marriage vows. Never safe, even after thirty years.

Some birds were monogamous, but most mated and split up. Birds do it. Let's fall out of love.

He wondered if he would ever find someone he wanted to marry. His girlfriend at
the moment was a fellow graduate student
in ornithology, though she was thinking of
becoming a vet instead. He liked her, but
he certainly didn't want to marry her. Or
anyone right now. Of course, his father had
asked him if he was seeing anyone. Of
course, Brian said no. Out of spite, he supposed. Though at the time it felt more like
simple manners, protecting himself and
Cynthia from his father's intrusive curiosity.

He walked slowly to his aunt and uncle's
house. It had seemed so far from his house
when he was little. Everything in town
seemed smaller now. Except his cousins.
When he thought of Daphne and Laurel
with their red hair and superior knowledge
of the world, two skinny girls towering over
him, he felt as though he were still a child
and always would be.

He remembered walking in the woods so
many years ago, walking with the superior
cousins, listening to them speak in code. He
remembered thinking, I'll show them. And
he did. He literally showed them what he
could see and they could not. He showed
them an ovenbird on the edge of a stream.
They shrugged.

Then he said, *"Seiurus aurocapilla."*

They stopped and Daphne pulled out her notebook to write down the words.

"It's the scientific name for ovenbird," Brian said. "Their nests are shaped like ovens. In a dome."

He had memorized the Latin names of all the birds he saw. Some children liked baseball statistics or memorized the names of all the presidents. But Brian liked birds. And trees. And clouds. He liked the way they looked, the ways they changed but still were the same bird or tree or cloud. And he liked their names.

The twins nodded, though they were far more interested in the etymology than they were about seeing the delicate little bird with its spotted chest or hearing it singing, *"Teacher, teacher, teacher."*

But Brian had discovered the key to their attention. A cloud in the sky was of real interest to them only when they were told it was a cumulus cloud and that "cumulus" meant *heap* in Latin. In their way, Laurel and Daphne were as fatuous as his father, he had realized.

He wondered what he could say to them now that would impress them. Nothing. They would smile and pat his head and say how grown-up he was, but he would always be little Brian to them. Daphne was particularly insufferable these days, or he was envious of her success, or both. Laurel had retreated into perfect motherhood, which was its own insufferable showing off, he thought.

He stopped and watched some pigeons at the base of a trash can. How beautiful they were, iridescent in the clear sunlight. They were overlooked or considered vermin in most places, but it didn't seem to bother them. They puffed out their breasts and cooed like doves. Brian searched his pockets for crumbs. He usually carried dog treats in case he met a hostile dog on his birding expeditions, but there was nothing in these clean jeans.

"Sorry," he said to the pigeons.

"Coo, coo, coo," they replied. And Brian smiled and thought families were not so bad. They were like these pigeons, cooing and puffing up and scrapping for crumbs. Like every other kind of creature. He thought of throwing dog biscuits at his cousins to calm them, tame them, make them his friends, and that made him laugh and enter the house in a better mood.

He said all his hellos to the older generation, answered their questions about where he was in his graduate studies, yes, still another year or so, yes, he studied birds, their mitochondrial DNA, actually, no, it was the DNA that passed through the mother, blah, blah, blah, and blah.

He saw Michael and Larry — too deep in conversation to interrupt — but he did not see Daphne or Laurel anywhere. He wandered around the backyard, idly looking up at the trees for a flutter of some kind, then sat on a chair that had been set out and waited, as if he were in the field, for something to happen.

Which it did. A beautiful girl walked toward him, little Prudence clasping one hand, Charlotte the other. The girl looked familiar, a dramatic sort of person, a mass of dark wavy hair, pale skin, her cheeks flushed pink in the heat.

"You look familiar," he said after the little girls crawled into his lap. "Not you two. Your keeper."

She stared at him a moment, then said, "Flower girl."

He stared back at her. The shiny black ringlets, the big resolute eyes, the clouds of tulle. The defiance. She smiled grimly at him, as if to say, *Yep, that one.*

"The little girl in the fluffy *Gone With the Wind* dress?"

"Yep, that one."

"You've grown up," he said.

"I'll get over it."

She sat down on the grass. The girls climbed down from his lap and began to try to do cartwheels. She sighed heavily.

Brian said, "You sound miserable."

"I am. I come from a broken home."

"Really? Me, too! Those are my parents over there. Cordially chatting with each other."

He could think of no other words for the hypocritical pantomime he was seeing.

"They don't look divorced."

"It's a secret."

The flower girl laughed.

"I find them nauseating," he said.

The flower girl said, "Aren't you too old to find your parents nauseating?"

"Never too old for that."

He was still marveling at the transformation of the flouncing flower girl into this person, this human. "I remember you so well from the wedding," he said.

She grinned. "I made quite an impression, didn't I?"

They were both watching his parents now. Cordially chatting with Arthur and Sally.

"Do you think they're secretly divorced, too? Arthur and Sally?" the flower girl asked.

"Probably."

"Did your parents bribe you with stuff?"

"No. I actually am too old for that."

"That's too bad. I think bribery is fair in my case. It's very inconvenient to have divorced parents when you're growing up. They're trying to make up for that, and I appreciate it."

That sounded sensible to Brian, profound almost. He wondered if he could still put in his claim.

Daphne could see her father through the window of the small room that had once been a screened-in porch and then became the den filled with bookshelves. He was leaning back in his armchair, his eyes closed.

"Daddy?" She knocked at the open door. "How are you holding up?"

"I'm fine. Just taking a break. Just thinking."

"About what?"

"How much you girls loved this room, as a matter of fact."

"We did."

The books on the shelves were so familiar, the spines faded, the titles in worn, unreadable gold letters. She could feel herself, on her toes, reaching up for a book, feel the coarse cloth of the binding; the weight of the book as she tipped it toward her, sliding it from the high shelf. She wondered if her notebooks were still upstairs in the bedroom she'd shared with Laurel. She went to the dictionary on its stand, reached over, and let the pages riffle past her fingers.

"You and your sister loved each other so much. I can still see you two hunched over that dictionary together."

Daphne let her index finger pop down the niches in the side of the dictionary.

"A sister is always a sister," she said.

She and Laurel had ceremoniously handed their mother their gift, a cashmere sweater and a bunch of days at a day spa. There was a speech printed out, the paper folded in a deep, careful crease. They had written it together, over the phone. They unfolded it together. They read it in unison.

"We love you, Mom," they had said when the speech was finished. "Happy birthday!"

They had spoken in the first-person plural. They had spoken together. Their mother had gazed at them with love and gratitude, and they had turned to each other with a sudden, mutual rush of love, an embrace, a tear.

Then there was a birthday cake. It was a coconut cake, Sally's favorite, and *Happy Birthday Sally* was written on top in beautiful pink-icing script. One candle for each decade. Sally had ordered the cake and poked each candle into the icing herself. Arthur carried it out of the kitchen and into the backyard, the candle flames tall in the still summer air. Sally looked first at Laurel, then at Daphne. She made a wish and blew out the candles.

It was a wonderful party, Sally thought now, looking back, even if my wish did not come true.

MO´RTUARY. *n.s.* [*mortuaire,* Fr. *mortu-arium,* Latin.] A gift left by a man at his death to his parish church, for the recompence of his personal tythes and offerings not duly paid in his life-time.
— *A Dictionary of the English Language*
by Samuel Johnson

The dictionary is sprawled on its stand, open to pages 1072 and 1073 — "Goat God" to "Godden" to "Goddess" to "Going." Drawings of a "goatsucker" and a "goby" and a "godwit," two birds and a spiny-backed fish. *Webster's New International Dictionary of the English Language,* Second Edition, Unabridged. Unabridged except for the missing pages 75–76, on which would have been found the word "altar."

The altar. The dictionary dais Arthur had

drawn forth from the trunk of the Buick so many years ago. There it was, holy platform for the holy book of words. Whether you were "God-fearing" or you were "godforsaken," the dictionary's altar remained in the little den lined with big books, and the dictionary was open upon it. *God of love, god of war, god of wine,* you are all there on the silky pages, though you are lowercase. *Goddess of Liberty, Goddess of Mercy, Goddess of Reason,* you are all gathered together there, too, but you, somehow, have attained the glory of the uppercase.

But there is no god or God or goddess or Goddess, thought Laurel, spreading her palms on the sacred pages. Even the dictionary is arbitrary, trying to capture contingency, to enchain syllables, to lash the wind.

Going, Daphne read over her sister's shoulder. *Departure.*

Their father was gone.

On the plane from Indianapolis to New York, Brian leaned against the window and thought about the last funeral he had attended. He had described it as the Great Jewish Weep 'n' Eat to his mother, but she did not think it funny and he had realized instantly that neither did he. That was the funeral for his grandfather, a very old man.

302

But Arthur was not a very old man. And Brian put his face down on the tray in front of him, buried his face in his sweater, and cried.

It's not the end of the world, his chair had said when Brian told him he had to go to New York.

The end of the world was such an odd concept. The world ended for someone every day, every minute, probably every second. And still the world toddled along. Soon it really would end, in five billion years or so, if it didn't crash into something first. But humans would be gone long before that. Everybody dies, and the world will die, too. So why worry?

Everybody dies. But Uncle Arthur was not supposed to die yet.

The twins once told him they remembered when Grandpa had two real legs. They remembered him driving a Cadillac. They said that Grandpa always knew which girl was which, even when his mind was long gone. That's when Uncle Arthur said that when they were babies, when they were first born, their mother put nail polish on one baby's toe so they could tell them apart.

"Which baby?" the girls asked.

"How should I know?" Uncle Arthur said with a laugh.

Brian's mother was waiting for him at the airport gate, smiling, waving, hugging. When had she become such an exuberant person? He patted her head and said, "Down, Fido."

Paula opened the trunk and Brian deposited his little rolling suitcase. She wished it had been a big suitcase, a steamer trunk, filled with clothes for every season.

"I don't understand why you live in Indianapolis," she said.

"No. Neither do I."

"I mean, I do. Of course I do. Academia, academia. You go where you must."

She burst into tears. Brian put his arms around her. "Oh, Arthur," she said. "Arthur, Arthur, Arthur."

They drove through town, past their own house, toward the funeral home.

She stopped at a red light and turned to look, again, at Brian. What a fuss he used to make as a small child, how withdrawn he became as an adolescent, and how quickly and thoroughly he had moved away as soon as he could. But she only had to hear his voice to feel as close to him as ever. Don had been jealous, of course, and thrown an occasional bitter professional diagnosis her way because of that. But that was long ago. Don had mellowed, or she had, or both most likely. And now Arthur's sudden heart attack had put everything and everyone in a different light.

She had felt a deep family love for Arthur for what seemed like her entire life. The tension between him and Don was noticeable even the first time she met Arthur at a French restaurant. She had duck, she could remember that clearly, duck à l'orange, delicious. Sally was there. They wore Stevenson buttons. Or was that another dinner? Arthur said, "Welcome," and that's all it took for Paula to feel at home with him. Sally took her hand and shook it in a hearty, boyish manner, and Paula was at ease with her, too. They made people feel at ease, which was just as well with those two precocious wild things for daughters. Maybe that was what drove Don crazy about his brother, how at ease Arthur made everyone feel. She knew what drove Arthur crazy about Don — Don. He was like a snarling cur around Arthur. Well, the girls paid Don back tenfold, that's for sure.

Paula wiped tears away with the back of her hand. She had been twenty when she met Arthur, younger than her son was now, how odd. Time was odd.

Brian smiled at her and said, "Green light, Mom."

■ ■ ■ ■

Neither daughter was able to speak at their father's funeral. Their husbands read what they had to say while Daphne and Laurel wept. Sally was silent, dry-eyed, shocked. At the house that evening, Paula sat beside Sally, patting her hand. Daphne watched them and thought how long they had known each other and tried to remember what they always whispered and laughed about in the kitchen during those Sunday family get-togethers. She had eavesdropped — they had seemed to have so much fun in there — but the conversation turned out to be about nothing, about vacuuming dog hair, about the ladies' room at the courthouse, about politics, about the weather, about a *New Yorker* cartoon — about all the things everyone spoke of, yet it had been so intimate an exchange. They had spoken of nothing and everything in such mirthful tones. Privity, Daphne thought. That's what it was. Two people, separate and private if only for a moment, communicating. Like sisters. Like twins.

She watched Michael pile his plate with what she thought of as Dead Jew Food. Whitefish salad. Slightly stale rye bread.

Herring. It was raining outside and every window was closed against the wet, cold air. She saw her father, or the legs of her father stretched out, visible in the doorway of his den, but they weren't his legs at all. They were Don's.

She stood in the doorway and watched him. One hand stroked the tall pile of *New Yorker* magazines, the other covered his eyes. His body shook with sobs. Daphne approached him hesitantly, but he looked up and leaped to his feet, his hand knocking *New Yorker*s to the floor. Daphne bent to pick them up.

"He was a good man," Don said, a voice behind her, a voice too late for her father, but welcomed by her.

"Yes, he was."

They stood facing each other. Daphne clutched the magazines against her chest.

"I'm sorry," he said.

"Me, too."

Quiet filled the little room of books, but murmurs and bits of conversation floated in from other parts of the house. They're just words, Daphne thought. Meaningless words that don't change anything. My father is dead.

There were no words for what she felt, the depth of the emptiness, the breadth of the emptiness, the emptiness of the emptiness. Words could only cloak what she felt. Words were supposed to illuminate and clarify. Words were meant to communicate information and feelings from one person to another. But today words stood numb and in the way. We are alone, Daphne thought, words can't change that. And our lives are as meaningless as a single, lonely letter, an *s* with just a hiss that meant nothing, a *p* sputtered, a *t* of staccato disapproval. Today, every word seemed wooden, leaden, no distinction between wood and lead, just inanimate weight.

"Sometimes I hate words," she said. But Uncle Don had already left the room, and the sentence fell in the woods with no one but Daphne to hear it.

Laurel, too, found herself drawn to the study, the room Uncle Don had made fun of, the little library room that had once been a screened-in porch with spiders in the corner, her father's proud refuge, her playground with her sister and their pet words. She saw Daphne standing by their father's armchair, clutching some old magazines, looking lost — literally lost, as if she had taken a wrong turn in a strange forest. Laurel opened her arms, and Daphne walked into the embrace.

For a long time, neither of them could have said how long, they stood in the little library and held each other and wept, loud gasping sobs that were so loud and gasping they brought others to the door. But whoever looked in at the two sisters looked away, quickly, and moved on.

For a week, the traditional Jewish time of mourning, Daphne and Laurel spent each evening at the house they'd grown up in. On some nights, their husbands joined them and stood by the fireplace sipping Arthur's middling scotch and speaking in hushed voices. On two nights, the children came and played Monopoly in the kitchen. On all the seven nights, Sally occupied the chair in the living room that had been Arthur's favorite. She didn't want to see it empty. She received the condolences of her friends and family with a wan smile. She assumed she would die soon, too, though she did not speak of that. She did not want to be reassured.

On the seventh night, after the herring and egg salad and roast beef sandwiches had been distributed to visitors or put away in the refrigerator and all the glasses and cups had been washed and put away, Laurel and Daphne dried their hands on the dish towel they had brought back from a trip to France years ago. The Eiffel Tower, wet and wrinkled, was smoothed out and hung above the sink. They remembered a nightmarish hitchhiking episode in Provence they'd never divulged to their parents and marveled at their youthful insanity, then split a brownie and joined their mother, Michael, and Larry in the living room.

"If you drove to Bridgeport you could take the ferry to Port Jefferson and drive home via Long Island," Larry was saying.

"That would take, what, three extra hours?" Michael said, looking at his watch as if that would tell him. "But the ferry would be beautiful."

"Cold. But beautiful."

Cold but necessary, Daphne thought. Like numbers.

"Cold but necessary," Laurel said.

"Like numbers," said Sally. And finally, after more than a week since Arthur's death, she began to cry.

After what seemed like hours but was probably just a minute or two, Sally stopped. She accepted a cup of tea, pouring whiskey into it. She said, "He loved you girls so much. You and your words." She smiled. She said, "Oh, Arthur." She shook her head. She said, "When he would chase you, when you said, 'There are two of us'? And chanted it? And he would chase you all around the house?"

Yes, Daddy and his numbers allergy. They had so much fun teasing him. They loved the books he brought home. They remembered the day the dictionary arrived. It was like a sibling, they said. Like a little brother. Or sister. It was precious and it was part of him and always would be.

More tea was passed around. More whiskey. Aunt Paula's coffee cake on paper plates. The paper plates sagged beneath the weight of Aunt Paula's cake. Why had their mother gotten such flimsy paper plates?

"What's with these plates?" they both murmured, then looked at each other and said, "Ha!"

"Oh, Arthur, Arthur," their mother said softly into her cup of spiked tea.

"I'll take such good care of the dictionary," Laurel assured her.

Daphne said, "No, no, the dictionary will be much happier in Brooklyn."

"You can't have the dictionary, Daphne, that's crazy. I'm the oldest. It comes with me."

"That is completely unacceptable and you know it and Daddy would never want that for the dictionary. Never. He'd want it with me. I can consult it for my work. I can appreciate it in a way you can't."

"What about my work? I *create* things with words. I don't bully other people about their choices."

"Oh, right, create. That's a laugh. You appropriate, that's what you say you do anyway. 'Sample'! Like a rapper. Create? Wrong word, Laurel. Look it up."

The argument escalated quickly, noisily. Michael tried to distract Daphne with comments about Prudence, her homework, the long drive home. On his side of the boxing ring, Larry poured more scotch into Laurel's cup — perhaps she would pass out and he could sling her over his shoulder, like a beautiful, obstreperous thirties movie star, her little fists weakly pummeling his back.

Sally closed her eyes. The dictionary. The dictionary held the world between its covers. The world was shrunken and drab now without Arthur, but what there was of it the dictionary embraced with magnanimity. How delighted the girls had been the night the dictionary came, how thrilled Arthur was with the gargantuan thing on its throne, its altar. How silly the girls were being now, two grown women squabbling like the children they used to be. *Go to bed this instant!* she wanted to say. *Arthur! Tell them if they don't stop quarreling they will be sent to their room.* But there was no Arthur to back her up. There was only Sally, now, to back up Arthur.

"The dictionary stays," she said.

Some angry noises from her children. Some angry words. Many angry words. Words, words, words! I'm so sick of words, she sang to herself. But there were words that had to be said, there were always words that had to be said if there was anything to say and even when there wasn't. Her head was swimming from the whiskey and the grief and the rage at her quarreling children who were acting like children. She would have to act like their mother. They were fatherless now. They needed her more than ever, the two big redheaded baby birds, more like screeching birds of prey than twittering bluebirds.

"Girls!" she said.

They stopped.

"It was your father's dictionary," she said. "Now it is mine. Your father is gone, but I am still here. The dictionary is still here. It will stay here, where it belongs. On its stand. In your father's den."

"But —"

"I do not want to hear one more word on this subject ever again."

"But —"

"Not one word."

To Word. *v.n.* [from the noun.] To dispute.
— *A Dictionary of the English Language*
by Samuel Johnson

Sally did not hear one more word on the subject. Nor did her daughters exchange one more word in person. The possession of the dictionary remained the subject of bitter controversy, but Daphne and Laurel moved their quarrel to print. When Daphne's column targeted a respected journalist who had written "know of which he speaks" and, incredibly, "the up most confidence," the column also mentioned *Webster's* Second Edition, how cavalierly, arrogantly it had been usurped by *Webster's Third,* how relativism was slowly eating away at the very foundations of the culture. Another column centered on the sentence "The congressman has been accused by nearly ten

315

women," and Daphne asked whether that was nine and a half women, nine and three quarters women, or nine and one-thirtieth perhaps, and railed against imprecision in the world of letters and the world at large. The carelessness and ignorance of the writer in question was a symptom of a general carelessness and ignorance in language, a valorization of carelessness and ignorance, a lack of appreciation for tradition, all of which could be seen in the contemporary attack on the literary canon, the lowering of standards in published poetry and short stories, and the changes from *Webster's* Second to the loosey-goosey of *Webster's Third.*

Laurel, soon after, wrote a poem published in *The New Yorker* called "I'm a Sit Right Here." It was an obscure poem, but it seemed to have something to do with a large book.

Neither Laurel nor Daphne was famous in the way that celebrities are famous. No one recognized them on the street. They could not get restaurant reservations anyone else couldn't get. But in the world of words in New York, they were known, and they were known to be twin sisters. There was, therefore, an item about them on Page Six. The glamorous redheads, identical twins, mysterious feud, Brooklyn vs. Manhattan. The Rift was official.

Everyone close to them tried to calm them down. Aunt Beverly Hills called with a teary pep talk. Aunt Paula tried reason, Uncle Don guilt.

"This is all about your father," Uncle Don said. He started with Laurel, thinking she might be the more reasonable one. "This is a natural reaction to grief, this desire to blame someone. But your father would be so unhappy about this."

"My father was unhappy about a lot of things, wasn't he?" she said pointedly.

Don tried Daphne next. "Lashing out in your grief — your father would be so unhappy about this, Daphne."

"My father is dead, so nothing either of us can say or do will get back to him."

Mr. Gravit, who felt duty-bound to listen to Laurel's complaints after she had listened to so many of his during his divorce, was so disconcerted by the situation that he got in touch with Daphne's friend Becky to see if, together, they could do something to resolve it. They met at a midtown coffee shop for the sake of discretion.

"Daphne would kill me if she knew I was here," Becky said. She flagged the ancient waiter. "White wine. White toast."

Gravit ordered coffee and fruit salad.

"Is it fresh? The fruit salad?" Becky asked the waiter.

"Of course."

"Oh. Okay. Thanks. I only like canned fruit salad. So, Mr. Gravit, why are they torturing us like this? Have they no shame?"

"It's tiresome and tedious."

"Well said." She tasted the thick yellow wine. "I'm a sucker for coffee shop cuisine."

"My divorce was much more civil than this," Gravit said.

"Oh well! Did you read Daphne's column on the word 'civil'? It was a response to something Laurel wrote in a book review — a book review! — in *The Boston Globe.* This is not the nineteen-fifties, Daphne and Laurel. This is not *Partisan Review.* What are they thinking?"

Gravit looked across the table at her, her nicotine-stained fingers, her nicotine-colored dress, the smudge of ink on her chin.

"What is anyone ever thinking?" he said.

"I would say it's like a horror movie, hideous creatures roaring out of the womb, but I like horror movies, and I don't like this."

They sat in the booth of the coffee shop, Gravit sipping from the heavy coffee cup,

Becky sipping the heavy wine. With her fork she stabbed a piece of orange from Gravit's bowl of fruit salad.

"I actually *love* horror movies," she said.

Gravit thought, Yes, how like you. He pushed the fruit salad her way.

"Thank you. Do you like rye toast? With butter? I like that even more than horror movies. One of my favorite foods. But I think I like white toast better. It's a dilemma. Do you smoke?"

"I started again after my divorce," Gravit said, shamefaced.

Becky nodded. "You can never quit. It's a myth."

After their fourth weekly meeting to discuss strategy they stood on the sidewalk outside the coffee shop. "Ah, the irony," Becky said. The tips of their cigarettes glowed faintly in the streetlights of the city night. "Malice has brought us together."

"Cigarettes and malice," Gravit said happily.

As they parted, Becky could hear him singing, to the tune of an old Frank Sinatra song, "Suddenly I saw . . . cigarettes and malice . . . all around a pug-nosed dream . . ."

Sally said, to anyone who dared bring up the subject of the Rift, *At age forty-four,*

Laurel and Daphne have to grow up, but few dared bring it up. She was steely on the subject of the dictionary. "Not a word," she would say in a cold voice. "I am in mourning."

Sally was angry at death. She was personally enraged. Sometimes she shook her fist at death, wherever it was, doing what it did to so many innocent people everywhere on the globe, and especially Arthur.

She thought her daughters must be angry, too, and it broke her heart to imagine them feeling the emptiness she felt. They still had their husbands, but the loss of Arthur filled her life, and she believed it must fill theirs with the same amplitude of emptiness. Alone, without Arthur, she needed Daphne and Laurel, but she also felt she must protect them. Daphne and Laurel, who had always seemed to protect each other, even when they seemed to protect each other from each other. Now they were truly unmoored. No father, no twin to reflect the loss of that father.

It is up to me, Sally thought. The responsibility weighed on her, heavy and urgent.

At the same time, she gloried in the intimacy she had with her daughters. They made more time for her now, their widowed mother. Did they compete to be the most thoughtful, loving daughter? And if they did, was there anything wrong with that?

The afternoons with Daphne, hours of languid, friendly confidences, became a weekly Saturday tradition. On Sunday, she went to Manhattan to cook big dinners with Laurel, Laurel who had been spooked by eggs as a child. There was no sense trying to push either daughter toward the other. They repelled each other now, like magnets. But, she assured herself, the alienation between Laurel and Daphne would not last. How could it?

In the meantime, what was Sally supposed to do with all this rage, sickening waves of anger, her ears ringing with blood, her eyes aching with tears and ugly, stinging, swollen membranes of red rage?

I am lost in my own home, she thought. The modest house she had lived in for so long was cold and vast and unrecognizable, a desert of a house. The only thing recognizable sometimes was the dictionary open on its glossy wooden stand, an ungainly dun-colored creature balanced on one dark, shiny leg.

Paula called to see how she was holding up.

"I'm holding up," she said. But what was she holding up?

The winter light was so frail.

Arthur took me for granted, she thought. And I took him for granted. That is the point of marriage. That's what marriage is. And now she had no one to take for granted. Certainly not her daughters. They needed her attention now and her strength. She was King Solomon, but she would not offer to cut the dictionary in half. If she did, her children would only argue about which one should get the head, which the feet. She was King Solomon, but it was the twins who had to break apart in order to come together. King Solomon was even crazier than King Lear, she thought. King Kong, now, that was a king. Protective, loyal. Where was King Kong when you needed him? Her lab tests had not been great, and there was no king or ape or Arthur or Daphne or Laurel who could fix that. When she lifted a dish to throw, to make a noise in the emptiness, she noticed it was dirty, brown with the remains of lunch, an avocado salad. She carried the plate into the kitchen and washed it.

AFFLAT´US. n.s. [Lat.] Communication of the power of prophecy.
— *A Dictionary of the English Language*
by Samuel Johnson

Sally will never see the girls again. She will close her eyes and she will be gone. She will be in her bed at home, and then she will be gone. She sees what will happen through her closed eyes. She sees the scenes in words. Words are what she is made of, what the world is made of when you tell your tale or someone else's.

Daphne and Laurel will grow old, older than Sally ever will live to be. They will live in the same city, one on an island, the other on another island. Laurel in Manhattan, Daphne in Brooklyn, the western end of that glacial deposit called Long Island. They will not have spoken in years, ten years, twenty, maybe, thirty — Sally cannot be sure, the future is murky even to her, watching it in words behind closed eyes.

Michael will retire and spend most of his time sailing a small sailboat he keeps at a marina near Floyd Bennett Field. He sails in the nineteen-foot sailboat, which he shares with a friend, from April to November. In the remaining four months, he and Daphne travel. They go to Botswana and Japan and Bhutan. They hike, with many stops for whiskey tastings, in the Hebrides. They are insufferably bourgeois, they tell each other, finding that their admission somehow mitigates a life they would once have considered ludicrous. Daphne continues to write, though her syndicated column has suffered along with the newspapers that once carried it. She writes a blog for a while, but blogs go out of style, and her daughter helps her set up a language podcast. On the podcast, instead of writing about writing, Daphne talks about talking. She is funny and harsh and finds new, young listeners. I am a language scold and I like it, she tells Michael, not for the first time. He answers as he always does, as Laurel once did: You were born for the job.

Sally agrees: Daphne was born for the job. And Michael, she tells the darkness, was born for her daughter Daphne. She has always liked Michael, a man of uncompromising kindness to temper Daphne's uncompromising . . . Sally falters in her story made of words as the story searches for the right word. Daphne's uncompromising . . . uncompromisingness!

Michael is there, in the room, with Sally. He touches her hand with his hand. She remembers when he walked down the aisle with Larry, the two grooms in their feminist aviator glasses. She knows they will stay together as long as they live. She laughs inside her darkness because the words suggest that it will be Michael and Daphne who stay together, and they will, but what the words of her story mean is that Michael and Larry will stay together; and they will, too, until the day they die, which is not the same day, but close enough. Michael will fight a disease with good humor, and when Larry finally succumbs to congestive heart failure, Michael will be losing his good humor and will arrange for a cocktail of drugs that allows him to go quietly into his own darkness, much as he has helped Sally arrange to go quietly into hers. Michael will sell the boat a few years before this happens, he and his sailing partner. His sailing partner can no longer manage the strain of getting on and off the little sailboat. His sailing partner has gotten weak because of his congestive heart failure. Michael's sailing partner is Larry, of course, but no one knows it until they sell the boat and come clean.

In the darkness, Sally can see the words that make up this part of the story:

Larry will take a cab to Brooklyn to the marina to have one last look at the small fiberglass sailboat, a pretty robin's-egg-blue, its soggy lines coiled neatly. The centerboard (replaced five years ago), the engine (replaced ten years ago), the sails in their sail bags, the cold wind whipping through the bay, the mushroom-shaped ride at Coney Island in the distance. Michael will already be there. He has made a pot of linguini with clams, and he helps his old friend into the boat, where they sit across from each other and drink beer from cans. Michael dishes the linguini out of the enormous pot he has brought from home. A gull paces the dock, watchful, gigantic.

The boat is called *Without You.* The title of a song from *My Fair Lady.*

"I will miss this," Michael will say.

Larry will give a short wheeze in agreement.

Michael will sit next to him, hold up his phone, and take a selfie, two old men, their sparse hair ruffled by the wind, their eyes bright.

He will post the photograph on whatever the future iteration of Facebook will be, and will caption it: *Ahoy!*

Daphne will see the photo right away.

Laurel's daughter will point it out to her minutes later.

The twins will be furious. It is as if they have discovered their husbands having an affair.

"That's your sailing partner? That's Lorrie?"

"That's Mickey?"

It is an affair, in its way.

"You brought us together," Larry will say to his wife. "You and Daphne."

"That was before."

"You can't just demand that a friendship end. That's not the way friendship works. You know that, Laurel."

Larry is very ill by this time. He is weak. He has trouble breathing. Laurel will sit next to him on the sofa and put her head on his chest and hear the hard work going on in there.

"Wow," she will say. "All these years? Wow."

Daphne and Michael will have a louder discussion, Daphne weeping and slamming doors, opening them in order to slam them again.

"How dare you? How could you? Why didn't you tell me? This is treason. This is treachery. This is two-faced. This is perfidy. This is sedition."

This is why I didn't tell you, Michael will say. Because you would have erupted into a thesaurus of insults and theatrics, just the way you are now. Because you are irrational on the subject of your sister. Because Larry is my best friend.

And then Daphne will cry as he holds her, because all those things are true.

"But you're pretty weird, you have to admit," she will say. "Sneaking around in your little boat."

Michael will not admit even that.

"I admit nothing. I regret nothing."

"What was the name of the boat?" she will ask.

"That you will never know."

And she never will. Though Sally knows. It is part of the story, and it amuses her.

They will take care of each other, Sally had said when her daughters were about to embark on their double wedding. She said it to Arthur, her dear Arthur in his pajamas, baby-blue cotton pajamas with white piping, he wore the same style pajamas until he died. He said, I know that, but who will take care of their husbands? Sally meant each half of each couple would take care of the other half of the couple, of course. And vice versa. But in the story, looking back and looking forward, it is the husbands who will be the ones who will take care of each other. Michael and Larry will stay together until the very end, until death does them part. Daphne and Laurel will continue to elbow each other out of the way in the giant womb of the world.

Larry is in the room now, beyond her closed eyes. Always the gentleman, he holds her hand to his lips. He whispers his own words: I love you, Sally. If she could embrace him she would. If she could embrace them all she would. She embraces them with the words of the story that unfolds behind her eyelids. In the story, she reaches up with her last bit of strength and holds her son-in-law close, then her other son-in-law. Then her granddaughters, Charlotte and Prudence. Prudence will be a doctor like her father. Charlotte runs an assisted living facility, a fancy one, Sally spent some time there, there were resident dogs that made it more tolerable, and there was Charlotte, as passionate and bossy as her mother, as tender as her father. Sally lets the story lift her arms to hug all the people who love her, whom she loves. Even Brian is there with his wife, the little flower girl with the shiny black ringlets.

But where are the twins?

Are they outside the room arguing? Of course they are. Is it "hopefully" this time? They stand outside the room face-to-face, nearly identical nose to nearly identical nose. Are they staying outside the room in an attempt to protect her from the bitter drama of their silly endeavor to be independent of each other? Don't bother, girls. And don't worry, either. I can see the story unraveling from where I am even if you can't.

To WILL. *v. a.* [*wilgan,* Gothick; *pillan,*
Saxon; *willen,* Dutch.] 5. It is one of the
signs of the future tense; of which it is
difficult to show or limit the signification.
— *A Dictionary of the English Language*
by Samuel Johnson

Sally has written the dictionary into her will.
Her daughters will wonder if she did it to
shame them, which will be partially true.
But she has done it for Arthur, too. To
protect his smile as he watched the little
girls, cheek to cheek, shoulder to shoulder,
trying to read all the words in the world.
And partly, this codicil in her will is whim.
What is the good of dying if you cannot
indulge in a whimsical codicil to your will?

The dictionary will spend half the year on
the Upper West Side with Laurel, and half
the year in Brooklyn with Daphne. Sally

does not insist on which six months will be spent in which borough, that is up to the dictionary's guardians, who she is certain will do what is best for their charge.

And so, the dictionary and its stand make their way to Manhattan first, to a spacious apartment that is welcoming, happy to receive it. In six months to the day, the dictionary and its companion, the dictionary stand, are placed in the trunk of Michael's SUV and driven to their winter quarters, equally welcoming.

This will go on for years, it will become a traditional harbinger of the seasons, like the turning of the leaves or the first crocus. Laurel will look at the dictionary and think of her father and his instant library and her mother and her codicil, her will that was her final act of will. And she'll think of Daphne, the sister who once followed her around, letting her do everything first, waiting for her to try each new thing, then jumping in with confidence and abandon. How had they lived together for so long? How had they lived apart?

When Daphne helped Michael load the dictionary into the car to go back to its other parent, she said it was like stuffing a baby back into the womb. When the six months were up and the car returned with its cargo, she watched Michael pull the dictionary out and thought of her father the night the dictionary arrived at their house in Larchmont. She could feel Laurel beside her on the couch, their bare feet touching, their breathing audible only to each other.

"I think you miss your sister, Daphne," Michael said.

"Phantom pain."

But phantom pain is painful, and they both knew it.

Girls, Sally wishes she could say from behind her closed eyes. *I do apologize for the absurdist touch, but how does a mother communicate with children who look at words and read them but don't listen? The dictionary will travel back and forth until the day you are left alone by the men who love you. And then perhaps you'll listen. Then perhaps you will be able to hear each other. Laurel will be the one to suggest it, and not right away. The loneliness will take some time to seep into your bones, but it will. Your children will rally around you. Your friends, too. But neither of you has ever been alone. Some people are good at being alone. They like it, or so I've heard. But you have never been alone, and, frankly, it stinks at your age. Old dogs, etc.*

"You know . . ." Laurel will say when it's

again time to take the dictionary back to her apartment for its six-month visit, "you know, my apartment feels so big. It's so empty."

You can no longer leave this task to Michael or Larry. It is a transfer you will have to do yourselves.

"My house feels enormous. And there are so many steps," Daphne will say.

"The elevator is a merciful invention for old bags like us."

"Old bags carrying bags."

You will sit at a coffee shop and you will talk and you will remember each other. You will listen to each other, curious, attentive, to this person you barely know yet know so well.

And then Daphne and Laurel, the identical twin sisters with identical red hair now acquired from two different downtown colorists, will fall into their old ways. They will live together again. In a building with an elevator. They will have a spot in the living room for the dictionary on its altar. They will argue over how much salt to cook with and whether or not to put the knives in the dishwasher. They will argue about words and they will chat about words as if words were pets.

Sally smiles as she sees all this rolling out in

the time she doesn't have but they do. *You must know this already,* she wants to tell her daughters. *But you're so stubborn that the story will take time, years. That's how stories are in life. It's like reading the dictionary from cover to cover,* she wishes she could tell them.

They come into the room and sit, one on either side of the bed. They each take one of Sally's hands. Their hands do not touch, but Sally doesn't mind. *You don't have to touch to be touching. I am touched. You have always touched me, even when I felt so alone, when you were one.*

In Sally's story, at this very spot, there is a momentary sentimental shudder.

The word is "love," the story tells her, but she says, *No, that is nonsense.* "Love" is a four-letter word, the story says, but Sally says, *No, you are missing the point. There is no word, just words, lots and lots of them, a universe of words, galaxies of them.*

The story shrugs and continues with these words: Daphne and Laurel love each other. Sally does not bother to answer, for that is a given, that is essential, that is albumen and yolk and shell together. *Relax,* she would tell the story if the story cared to listen. *Relax and see what happens next.*

ACKNOWLEDGMENTS

First, foremost, fervently, and forever I would like to thank my editor, shepherd, and pal, Sarah Crichton, who is simply the best; Molly Friedrich and Lucy Carson, the dynamic duo, thank you; Kimberly Burns, dynamic dynamo, thank you; Jonathan Galassi, Lottchen Shivers, and everyone at FSG, thank you; Tommy Denby, revered son and linguist, thank you; word lovers of Twitter, especially Nancy Friedman, thank you; for the all-important pencil, thank you, Betsy Wildman; and for the room with the Assisi view, thank you, thank you, Art Workshop International. I was a bad copy editor long ago, and so to the many good copy editors everywhere I say, thank you, thank you, thank you, and please forgive the inevitable errors. My motto: I stand, corrected.

ABOUT THE AUTHOR

Cathleen Schine is the author of the internationally bestselling novels *The Three Weissmanns of Westport, The Love Letter,* and *The New Yorkers,* as well as *They May Not Mean To, But They Do,* winner of the 2017 Ferro-Grumley Award. She is a frequent contributor to *The New York Review of Books.* Her work has appeared in *Best American Essays, The Big* NEW YORKER *Book of Dogs,* and *Fierce Pajamas: An Anthology of* NEW YORKER *Humor.* She lives in Venice, California. You can find her online at cathleenschine.me.

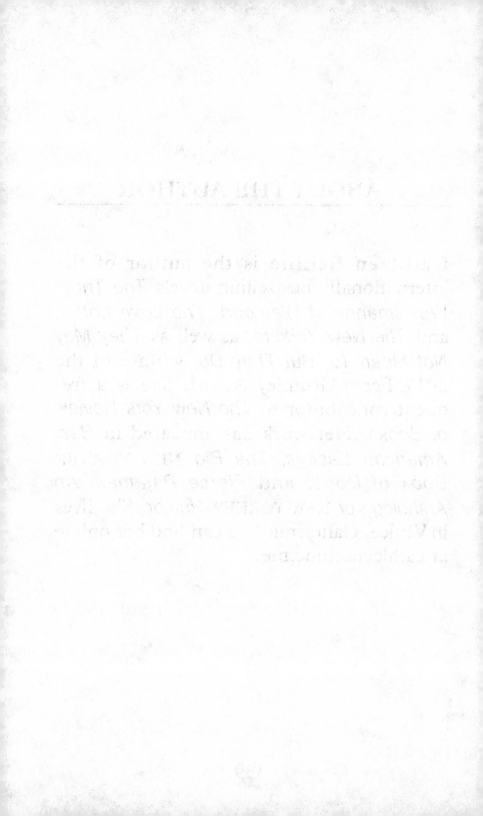

The employees of Thorndike Press hope you have enjoyed this Large Print book. All our Thorndike, Wheeler, and Kennebec Large Print titles are designed for easy reading, and all our books are made to last. Other Thorndike Press Large Print books are available at your library, through selected bookstores, or directly from us.

For information about titles, please call:
(800) 223-1244

or visit our website at:
gale.com/thorndike

To share your comments, please write:
Publisher
Thorndike Press
10 Water St., Suite 310
Waterville, ME 04901